THE RESERVATION

TASK FORCE E: BOOK ONE

JASON RUBIS

SEVEREDPRESS

TASK FORCE E: THE RESERVATION

This novel is a work of fiction. Names, characters, places and incidents are the product of the author's imagination, or are used fictitiously.
Any resemblance to actual events, locales or persons, living or dead, is purely coincidental.

ISBN: 978-1-923165-02-1

PROLOGUE

ALASKA, 1975

They found the man's wife late in the day, just as the sun was disappearing over the mountains. The man was in no condition to accompany the search team. He had been airlifted into a hospital in Fairbanks and asked everyone who came near his bed if his wife had been found yet, repeating the words like a recording. They put him out before the news was finally delivered—they had to; he couldn't have made it through the necessary procedures without sedation. It wasn't until he woke the next morning that anyone answered him.

"Where is she? Where's Barbara? Did they find any tracks? Any sign of what got her?"

An older man stood beside his bed, an expensive raincoat folded over his arm. He was staring down at him with an expression between concern and something like repugnance. His heavy mustache hid the reflexive chewing he was giving his upper lip.

"Where...?"

"She's gone," the older man said shortly, walking to the window and looking out over the early morning view of the city. "There wasn't anything left of her to save. But you knew that before they brought you in." His voice was full of distaste. "As for what did it, they think it was a bear. A grizzly, probably."

"No, not a bear," the man whispered, shaking his head savagely, as though the very idea was the height of absurdity. "Monsters. Bigger than the two of us put together." He lifted his bandage-wrapped hands, indicating something of immense size. "And vicious," he spat. "Like devils out of hell. Worse than anything you read about in the magazines, or those idiot documentaries." His eyes looked unfocused, haunted. "I knew I'd find them," he said, seemingly to himself. "I knew it."

"Why did you take Barbara with you, Jake?" the older man snapped. "Why the hell did you go there in the first place? And, don't give me your crazy bullshit about lost races and abominable snowmen. You as good as killed her yourself with your nonsense."

Trent turned his head and looked at the other pityingly. "You could have at least spared Barbara, Jake. She worshipped you, you bastard."

"You don't know," the man asked, turning his head onto his shoulder and looking at Trent like a broken doll. His expression was oddly peevish, like a sullen child. "You're not a believer, why the hell am I talking to you?"

He turned to look up at the ceiling. "You can leave," he said. "Just tell a nurse I want to see whatever doctor they've assigned me. I need to get out of here. I've got work to do...I have to make plans. You'll have to go to Switzerland for me this month, take care of the Henderson nonsense."

"You've got a bell, use it," Trent said. "I'm out. And I won't be going to Switzerland or anywhere else on your behalf. I no longer work for you...in any capacity. Understand that? No more fetching and carrying. I'll be in touch with Barbara's family. I'll leave it to you to do the decent thing and contact them...or have your secretary call them, more likely."

"You're leaving your stocks, then," the man said, suddenly sly.

"To hell with the stocks *and* you," Trent snapped. He shook his head. "God have mercy on you, Jacob." He went out, shouldering his raincoat on as he went.

The man lay quietly, moving his lips as he stared ahead. There was no one to hear him, but he was singing "A Mighty Fortress is Our God."

After a time, he stopped. "I knew it," he said, licking his lips. "I knew I'd find them."

ONE

Smithy dreamed about the lights again.

This dream, like all the others, had the peculiar effect of collapsing time, burning away all the years that came after. He wasn't Smithy at all in the dream; he was still just First Lieutenant Nat Smith, eighteen years old and just as green as hell. The others weren't any older or more experienced; they barely knew each other, having been airlifted in from various corners of the US and plopped down in a barracks. They were still shy with each other, but still dying to prove themselves, even though back then they weren't any better than kids playing soldier. *Boys*, Wizard would later say of their earlier selves, smiling a little.

That night, the night Smithy was dreaming about, the five of them were moving through a night-shrouded field in Montana. The field belonged to a rancher named Clemson Bartlett, and the spot they were moving toward was at the exact center of his property, though they wouldn't learn that till later. When the boys reached the spot, they stood staring at each other, shifting unloaded rifles from hand to hand. Flatfooted in their fatigues and muddy boots, unsure of what to do next.

They didn't feel like heroes. They weren't even ROTC; lately that fact had begun to rankle. US Defense Reserve Corps was the organization that had snatched them away before they'd had a chance to make up their minds. The recruiter had been a genuine four-star general, and he'd told each and every one of them they had a unique opportunity before them: not just an automatic scholarship to the university of their choice, not just military careers upon graduation, but the chance to serve their country in a unique and unusual way.

The problem was, he never told them exactly *how* they would serve, or in what way it was unique and unusual. Worse, it had quickly become clear nobody knew what USDRC really was, or even what branch of the Services it belonged to. Everybody knew the Marines, the Coast Guard, the Navy…they damned sure knew what the Army was, especially impressionable girls. Smith had dug into the internet via his school's computer library before he left his mom's home in North Carolina, just Googling his brains out—and got zilch for his efforts.

First Lieutenant Smith looked his companions over glumly. His older, sleeping self took in their faces with pleasure, wondering how in hell they could have ever been so young. Except for Wilson, they were all First Lieutenants. Wilson, who had been recruited before any of them, was Captain, and their leader for this maneuever. At least he wasn't an asshole, something Smith had been worried about. He was a jug-eared, soft-spoken fellow, but something about him made the others comfortable, gave the impression he knew what he was talking about and could be trusted. When he said, "Run," they ran. When he said "Down" they flopped down on their bellies and kissed dirt. No questions asked.

Lucian Evermore was black, tall with deep-set eyes that never seemed to miss a beat, and a deep voice. Graham Albrecht was heavily built, a ginger-haired Boston native who, despite his lack of height and good-humored, almost impish demeanor, looked like he might be a formidable fighter. Jesus—JessMaldonado was Filippino. Smith had thought he was either Mexican or Chinese, and had been mildly corrected the night they met. He kept fingering his stubbly crewcut with the air of missing something. He was from somewhere in California and liked talking about punk bands. It seemed like a strange background for someone bound for a military career; Smith gathered that Jess, like most of them, had joined the Corps mainly at the behest of his parents. None of them were rich, and it was their best chance for a college education, if not the actual career Flynn had promised them.

Their orders had just been to get to this spot. They'd had the idea there would then be *action* of some kind; another squad to engage with, or *something*. But there was nothing out here but cold open space and cow pats; Bartlett ranched cattle, but the animals were all put up for the night, their smell lingering in the cool air. No crickets. *The silence was deafening*, Smith would say later.

"Now what?" That was Albrecht, and it was the only thing Smithy remembered anyone actually *saying* in the dream. Maybe because it was what they were all thinking. If any of them had answered, it would have been with the same note of paranoia rising in their voices. This manuever was supposedly just an exercise, not much different from the yahoos who went out in the woods on weekends shooting each other with paint-guns. Sure. They'd all have a good laugh, then go back to the barracks. They had been promised a week's leave later; in that time, they'd be on the bus, bound for home and some good home cooking. But somehow this exercise had changed into something else. Maybe something a little more dangerous. Maybe something a little suspicious.

Smithy remembered Evermore shaking his head, like, *Man, I don't like this. I don't like this a'tall.* Maldonado was looking from one to the other; he had proven himself probably the most aggressive of them, even more so than Albrecht, but right then he put Smith in mind of a dog who smelled something dangerous out in the dark. Any minute he'd start whining, snarling if you got too close. Captain Wilson was looking around, sucking his teeth, looking more nervous than any of them.

Then the lights came, and everything went to hell.

As always, this effectively marked the end of the dream. Everything had been leading up to that point, falling towards it like ants tumbling down into an ant-lion nest, ready to be sucked dry. There was nothing now but the lights flashing, searing his eyes dry, and an impossibly fast-moving parade of images snapping by, as starkly uncomplicated as those in a textbook, as surreal as something from a horror movie. Animal-images, but not like anything you saw in the zoo: teeth, leather wings, rolling white eyes...

The jaws that bite, the claws that catch...

And that was it. Smithy's eyes snapped open and it was twenty years later. He was lying in the utter darkness of his cabin, and the sound of someone banging on his door, making a lot of noise about it. It didn't sound like the sound either knuckles or fists would make; it sounded as though someone were slapping his door open-handed, daring someone to do something about it.

There were other noises, too; loud snufflings, grunts and streams of barely-human babble some sources termed "samurai chatter." It would have been funny if the sounds hadn't been so hair-raisingly strange, like gossip you'd hear in Hell.

Smithy kept a loaded rifle on the floor next to his hard, narrow bed, right by his boots. He picked it up now before heading to the cabin's door. He was whistling through his teeth, pretending to be cheerful, pretending he wasn't sick to his stomach with apprehension.

The Old People seldom came to him, but when they did, it was rarely good news.

***

The guys who had hired Brick for a safari had come up from Johannesburg, three students from Witswatersrand hot to spend *pappa's* money. American kids were pretty bad, in Brick's estimation, but these yobbos seemed more than ready to give them a run for their money. They had brought a case of beer along and had started popping cans well before the land cruiser was half an hour from the lodge. At least they hadn't brought anything harder—that Brick knew of. The biggest and loudest of the guys—the one Brick called Daniel Boone—had spent a lot of time in the men's room back at the lodge, and he was wiping his nose a lot, sniffing like he didn't care who heard it.

Coked-up rich kids, drunk off their asses, hard as hell to see a thing they thought didn't even exist. Nice.

"Hey Boss," Daniel Boone shouted, in his South African accent—not unlike British, but breathier. "Boss! When we getting there, eh? To *Ground Zero*?" He was standing up in the vehicle, head poking up through the open top, trying to drink as they jolted along. Between the wind tearing his words away and making him choke on his suds, Brick could barely hear him.

"When I say we're there," Brick shouted back. "Now sit down and shut up." That got them laughing. Kids always liked Brick; he looked enough like a tough guy to give them someone to practice their little macho routines on, and just laid-back enough not to threaten them. Reynolds, the guy who booked his safaris, told him more than once that he should move to Africa. "Forget all the other languages, Graham. Learn just three words of Afrikaans, and you'll be golden. I can teach you right now: *braai, bier* and *koeksisters.* All you need."

He'd thought about the offer more than once. Truth was, he kind of liked Africa—or at least Kenya. It was sun-drenched, dry, bleak—*just like me.* With his heavy, compact build and his broad, broken-nosed face he looked right at home down here. The cities were shit, but with his business who needed the cities? He'd do alright out here in the grasslands. He liked the people too; just enough of a sense of humor but they weren't always trying to be your buddy or play Moriarty to your Holmes, like in the States. The asshole ratio was pretty low.

"Hey Boss!"

Brick cringed, trying not to let it show. *Then again...*

"I swear to God, Daniel Boone..." More laughs. Giving customers cute nicknames didn't always fly down here, but the pups seemed to liked it.

Hands tried to pull Daniel Boone back into his seat, but he didn't let up. "When we gon' see the monsters, Boss?"

Oh, Jesus. Brick pulled a squashed handful of Kleenex from his pocket, and slashed it over his streaming forehead. "The monsters will find *us,* don't worry."

At least "monsters" sounded slightly less cringey than "cryptids," which was what would be painted on the cruiser's sides if this were the States. But why had the question given him that little taste of freakout? This was a routine trip, easy-peasy-one-two-threesy. The kids were paying for all the extras: accommodations at the lodge, including drinks and meals, a night sampling the delights the nearest craphole to pass as a city had to offer. By the time Reynolds and the drivers took their share, he'd still be able to pay two months of rent plus maybe a decent carousing in town. He should have been relaxing. But he felt jumpy as a cat.

"What is it, though? The animal we're going to see?" That was the one he'd named Nayland, for Nayland Smith, the youngest and probably the least irritating of the bunch. Old Nayland had actually read a book or two. He leaned his skinny frame up into the front seat, between Brick and the driver. "People say it's a relict *chalicothere*."

That tickled Brick. Not the idea, but the slightly pompous way Nayland put it out there. Kid had been watching too much Animal Planet. Wizard would have got a kick out of him. "Do you even know what a *chalicothere* looked like?"

Nayland looked hurt. "Sure. It was related to giraffes, but it looked..." He shook his head, dazed with the wonder of the strange thing in his head. "It looked like a mix-up of horse and gorilla...walked on its knuckles."

"Right," Brick nodded. "It was weird enough lookin', that's true. But the *chemosit* ain't no chalicothere, 'relict' or extant or however you want to say it."

"How d'you know?" Leatherstocking challenged. Best-looking of the bunch, big light-skinned kid with muscles on his muscles...so of course he was the most irritating—and got the stupidest name. Leatherstocking wasn't as in-your-face obnoxious as Daniel Boone, but he had a way of getting his licks in right when you weren't expecting them.

Brick knew he should just either ignore the kid or give him crap right back ("Your mama told me before I threw her out last night"). But that nervousness was getting worse by the minute, for some reason. He didn't really think this was going to amount to more than passing off some hyena scat as *chemosit* shit; maybe if they were really lucky they'd glimpse something off in the distance he could convince them *might* be something stranger than it should be. Dr. Al's Monster Safari almost never came even to *that*.

But...

"I'm the guide on this enterprise," Brick said, scowling over his shoulder. "You all signed papers agreeing to that. This might be a good time for a reminder. I lead, you follow, that's the end of it. You keep that in mind, we may all get home tonight with all our arms and legs intact. And if you don't..."

"Shit!" That was from the driver, a hard looking Kenyan named Samuel. He hit the brakes hard, nearly throwing Brick out of his seat. The guy sat staring at something just ahead. He didn't look scared, exactly, but Brick noticed he wasn't getting out of the cruiser. He sat with his nostrils flared, eyes fixed on the thing before them: a huge mountain of something black and unmoving, streaked with shiny blood and ragged patches of ruby flesh.

Water buffalo. A dead one.

"Jeesus," Nayland breathed, climbing out of the land cruiser. "Look at its *head*, man!"

Yeah. Look at it. It looked as though a king-sized Freddy Krueger had torn the top of the buffalo's head clean off and scooped out the grey matter inside like so much ice cream. It had left one eye staring at the grass; where the other should have been was an empty, bloody socket. The lolling tongue was furred with blackflies.

Not good.

"Everybody just stay put," Brick hollered. He caught the driver's eye. "We need to go back to the lodge. Now." Samuel looked calm, but he nodded emphatically, letting Brick know just how good an idea that sounded. He muttered something that sounded like *"Duba."*

"Shit, man, this is what we came for!" Daniel Boone cried exultantly. He and Leatherstocking were making their way over to the dead buffalo, just a little unsteady on their feet. Leatherstocking aimed his phone and started firing off pics, probably destined for his buddies back in Johannesburg.

"No pictures! I said stay, in the, fucking *cruiser!*" Brick bellowed. He got Daniel Boone by the wrist and swung him back towards the vehicle. The force behind the swing must have startled him; he gave Brick a startled, comical stare, but said nothing as he sat back down. Then Brick turned to Leatherstocking.

"Party's over. This just turned serious. You want your money back, you got it, but we ain't staying here." This could go one of two ways now. Either the kid would realize they were up against something much bigger and uglier than they'd expected or...

"*Voetsek,*" the kid spat. *Fuck you.*

Okay, Brick thought, inhaling. *I guess we know which way we're going here.*

He could tell Leatherstocking was going to take a swing before he had even slipped his phone back into his pocket. He let him, taking the blow upside his cheek. Not bad, for a pup. There was some heat behind it. But it wasn't enough to knock Brick over, or, more importantly, erase the situation.

Brick drove his fist into Leatherstocking's gut, hard. He didn't want to do any serious damage, but he couldn't help but take a certain mean satisfaction in the kid's *whoomph* of released breath, the sudden widening of his eyes as he suddenly bent double. If nothing else, maybe he'd walk away from today with the knowledge that youth and a gym membership didn't automatically buy you stamina and endurance. If *any* of them walked away, that was…

"Come on," Brick said, extending a hand. He was already regretting his loss of control. The kid deserved it, but as the guide, Brick should have handled himself better. Leatherstocking took his hand long enough to pull himself upright, then shoved his foot against Brick's and pulled harder, trying to yank the other man over. Bush-league judo. Not smart. Brick was far enough past his initial surge of anger that he settled for pulling the kid close with a threatening glare.

"We don't got time for this," Brick grated. "There's something out there could kill all of us, do you get that, Peter Pan?"

That was when Nayland Smith began yelling. Brick looked up, and there it was, running at them at speed, slavering.

Chemosit. Kerit. Freaking *Nandi Bear*.

"Ah, hell," Brick grunted, all thoughts of Leatherstocking now totally forgotten.

Time to go to work for real.

***

The Old People were gathered around the cabin, standing in a wide semicircle, waiting for Smithy to show his face. It was dark, but the moon was full; he could make them out in its light, and there were plenty of them. Several clans' worth. They quieted their whooping and chatter as soon as they heard the door creak open. Smithy was calm as he stepped out into their midst, lantern in one hand, rifle in the other. The sight of the gun, as always, was enough to discourage them from doing anything stupid. He'd never shot one, never had to. He didn't expect to use the rifle tonight either, but...

The crowd included children, and those were the ones Smithy most studiously avoided. He could remember when this generation had been born; the clan females had brought them to the cabin to show him, like he was a tribal elder whose approval meant something. They were cute when they were little. But by now the smallest of the younglings could have uprooted a young ash, or twisted its trunk in two with a quick wringing motion. And as they got older, they were getting more aggressive, females as well as males. The males had their tusks already and a few of them were tussling on the outskirts of the crowd, growling and swatting each other—it was probably meant as playfulness, but one of those hard, thick-skinned paws could leave you without a face.

As for the adults, he was careful not to meet their eyes. The smallest of them went head-for-head with him, and he was considered pretty tall. Three of the adults, a female and the male he called Broken Tusk, came shuffling up to him, and he managed to snatch a quick breath so he wouldn't inhale the stink that surrounded them like an eye-watering cloud. Days-old carrion, sulfur, a dumpster left to ferment in the August sun; the Old People didn't seem conscious of the reek that was one of their most unique features.

Broken Tusk stared down at him with beady red eyes. His face reminded Smithy of the rubber gorilla masks they used to sell in the back of comic books, but scarier.

Smithy nodded at him, as though he were a neighbor come to pass a little time while the Mrs. fixed dinner. "Evening," he said. They had no common language, but he had found they responded well to simple, direct speech; better than most humans, really. He tried not to inhale, but he got a lungful anyway…and in it was a whiff of something else, something that made him frown.

The Old People's presence was sharpening his senses, as it always did. Years before, he would probably not have noticed the strange smell. Now he did. Except it wasn't really strange; it was all too familiar.

Somewhere in this dark crowd was another human being.

And as soon as he realized that, he saw him, walking slowly between two younger males, who glared down at him as though sending a silent warning not to run. Smithy lifted his lantern.

He didn't recognize the man. He was a little below normal height, in his late forties, maybe, balding and a bit on the chubby side. His outfit was right out of the L.L. Bean middle-aged hiker catalog. He blinked, lifting a pudgy hand to shield his eyes from the light. "Mr. Smith?"

"Haven't been called that in a long time," Smithy said. The words didn't come easily to him;

too long away from his own kind. Or maybe someone knowing his real name was getting just a little too close for comfort. He found himself forcing a cough to hide his mumbling.

The man nodded. "Smithy?"

"Better. But I haven't heard that one in a while either. You got me at kind of a disadvantage, mister."

"I'm Martin Bloom," the man said. He extended a hand and when Broken Tusk growled, he withdrew it.

"Your, ah, friends found me blundering around the woods. They seem very protective of you."

"More like protective of themselves. They don't like visitors. Visitors are a problem, see. Time was, they found a visitor, they'd just make him disappear. Easy solution. One with lots of good protein in it. But they've gotten to think of me as their problem-fixer, see. They'd rather I make the problem go away than them, even if it means they don't eat that night."

The little man nodded at the rifle in Smithy's hands, looking weary rather than frightened. "Is that what you're going to do now? Make me go away?"

"Nope," Smithy said, shaking his head. "'Cause, see, what I know that they don't is that kind of problem-solving just leads to more visitors, and more sooner than later. And I have to confess I'm a little curious as to what brings you out all this way. So, I think what I'm going to do by way of an alternative, Mr. Bloom, is invite you in for a cup of coffee. Hope you like it on the cold side. Got most of a pot left, but I live without electricity and I can't afford to waste what little java I have."

"Sounds fine to me," Bloom said, exhaling a breath. He glanced at Broken Tusk, and when the big male didn't make a move, he took a step towards Smithy. One step led to another, and in no time at all the cabin door squeaked again, this time shutting.

The crowd of Old People dispersed only gradually, as though suspicious Smithy might burst out at any moment with his rifle blazing. The younglings were the first to go, followed by their elders. Broken Tusk, hanging behind a moment, flung back his head and let out a scream before he shuffled back into the night.

It sounded oddly like a warning.

TWO

It wasn't just the animal's ferocious appearance that frightened Brick. *Chemosits* were normally nocturnal, creatures of the twilight like most African cryptids. Truth was, he had never seen one by daylight, let alone the harsh glare of early afternoon. For this one to be hunting humans now was unnatural, worrying—apart from the fact that it was almost close enough to bite his nose off.

It was easily the size of an adult rhinoceros, but not so bulky; its appearance—the shaggy reddish fur, narrow clawed feet and sloping back suggested both a hyaena and a bear. It wasn't either, though. The fanged mouth opened too wide, scrunching the eyes to fiery slits and flaring the nostrils, giving the thing's face a weirdly simian appearance. Brick had always suspected the things had their origins in primates, as if a particularly large and savage baboon had decided to give some other shape a try. Like, *let's try a ground sloth. A really* mean *ground-sloth that can run like a motherfucker and has a taste for brains.*

Samuel had seen enough. He was putting the cruiser in reverse, flying backward away from the thing before skidding round in a semicircle and taking off. Only Daniel Boone was along for that ride; Nayland Smith was running pitifully after them, squalling like a lamb as the land cruiser maneuvered, as though the driver were deliberately playing a sadistic game with the boy. Leatherstocking crouched on the ground, staring open-mouthed at the thing that was almost on them.

Brick ran to the right, ignoring the departing land cruiser. He didn't really blame the driver for running; besides that, the vehicle offered no real safety; the *chemosit* could run it down without even trying.

"Brain-eater!" he yelled, waving at the thing. "*Kerit*! *Koekkola*! Hey!" It was important to name them, even if they were just Category One or Two. Let them know from the outset you had their number—even though in most cases that was more for your benefit than theirs. The thing stumbled to a halt and turned its grotesque face on him, growling deep in its throat. Something told it that the screaming man was far more of a threat to it than the youngling cowering in the dust.

This is it, Brick. Time to go bye-bye. He was basically unarmed. He had a knife sheathed in his boot, but that was mainly to look cool for the customers. Against this monster, it'd be less than nothing, unless maybe he could trick it into swallowing the blade. Samuel kept handguns in the cruiser in case of serious trouble, but by now they were long gone. Brick could hear Daniel Boone howling in the distance, demanding they turn back for his friends.

The monster moved slowly towards him, its high shoulders lifting and falling. Brick stood with his hands outstretched, as though they were deadly weapons.

He tried desperately to think. How did they used to do it? Back when it was four of them, not just him? There were maneuvers they used, tactics that put the things off their guard. But what the hell were they? He couldn't remember.

A sudden realization came to him as he stared at the monster. *It's hungry. Starving.* Brick could feel the emptiness in the creature's belly growling in his own. *It hasn't eaten in days, but it's not weak yet. It's going to take its time...*

A clod of dirt flew out of nowhere, hitting the *chemosit's* shoulder. Leatherstocking was on his feet, gabbling and waving his arms. Brick winced. *No, no...don't try to save* me, *you idiot, run!* But testosterone was doing its work; Leatherstocking was going to either save Brick or go down with him. The monster growled and switched its attention back to the boy. Sooner or later, it would tire of games and just pick one to tear up first.

Don't think the two of us will be much of a meal for a brain-eater.

Then a vast shadow blanketed the three of them; shadow and a loud rhythmic noise Brick hadn't heard in quite a while: choppers.

There were two of them, sleek black birds that looked like they could move as easily and quickly as mosquitoes. They touched down with surprising speed and gentleness, and men in in padded black uniforms leapt out, their faces made invisible by convex shields, bulky rifles held close to their chests.

Warlords with private armies weren't unknown in this part of Africa, but Brick didn't recognize either the uniforms or the weapons. The guns weren't regular MKs; a thin humming noise surrounded the men and Brick had a feeling it was coming from the rifles.

This ain't necessarily good, but it's probably at least going to be interesting.

The *chemosit's* baboon-like head swung from side to side, trying to get the measure of this new threat. It didn't like this at all. It was used to stalking in the shadows, making easy meals of the occasional herder or a village woman who'd unwisely decided on a moonlit tryst with her boyfriend. Brick and the boy forgotten, it rose up on its hind-legs and shuffled—awkwardly but with menacing purpose—towards the army.

One man stepped forward, aimed his gun at the creature, and fired. There was a startlingly loud noise, like an ear-hurting burst of static, and the beast was suddenly enveloped in a net of crackling blue flames. The rest happened very quickly; really, Brick thought, it was almost anticlimactic. The *chemosit* screamed, a full-throated bellow of pain, and it fell heavily onto its side, raising a cloud of dust. After an additional moment of crackling, the flames died away.

And that was it. If the *chemosit* weren't dead, it was definitely out of commission for a while. The black-suited men set on it, unwinding rope from coils attached to their belts and speedily tying it up.

"Who are these guys?" Leatherstocking demanded, moving to Brick's side. "Hey, Boss…do you know?"

Brick shook his head silently. He was keeping an eye on the men. One—the man who had fired on the *chemosit*—stood apart from his fellows, watching them bind the creature. Then he turned to Brick, pulling a card from a section of his belt. "Dr. Albrecht," he said, briefly nodding as he offered Brick the card. His voice seemed to be filtered through his mask, which gave it an oddly metallic overtone.

Brick took the card. It was like a business card, but made of some kind of thin, inflexible metal. There was a name on it, JACOB STONE, and a phone number, the letters and digits stamped into the metal. Whoever had designed the card had made it to last.

Jacob Stone. The name felt familiar, but Brick didn't think it was anyone he knew personally. A celebrity or some kind of public figure, more likely. When he looked up the uniformed man had rejoined his colleagues. Brick didn't think he was Stone, for some reason.

"Boss," Leatherstocking persisted, sounding ready to tug at Brick's sleeve like an impatient five-year-old. Brick was too busy watching the men. A couple had piled back into one of the 'copters. The bird started up moments later and lifted off the ground. Before it got too high, one of the men hooked a rope attached to the bound *chemosit* to the railings. It lifted the creature slowly, and turned, gaining altitude. Soon it was headed north. The man who'd given him the card followed the others into the remaining 'copter. Soon it was following the first. Moments later all that was left of the encounter was a slightly flattened spot on the grass, where the creature had fallen.

"Boss!" Leatherstocking cried, giving Brick a solid, though not aggressive, punch in the arm.

"Okay, okay," Brick said, pocketing the card. "You still got your phone?"

"Yeah, but who *were* those guys? And that thing...was it really a Nandi Bear?"

"Answer number one, I have no idea. Answer number two, you bet your sweet patootie it was. And if you were going to try for a number three, just refer to number one. And get the lodge on your phone, would you? I'll talk to them, get us another vehicle out here. It's a long walk back, and I don't know about you, but I'm not in a walking mood right now."

***

"So, what is it that brings you up here, Mr. Bloom?" Smithy sat down at his kitchen table, a rough but sturdy construction of logs and boards. Besides the equally rough chairs, the woodburning stove and a heavy well-stocked bookshelf, it was all the small kitchen had in the way of furnishings. Bloom took one of the mismatched mugs of coffee Smithy offered. Smithy knew damned well the stuff tasted like crap, but the man drank half of it off as though thirst or a need for caffeine trumped any other consideration. He set the mug on the table and said, "Let's not play games, alright? May I call you by your given name?"

"Rather you didn't."

"Smithy, then. I didn't mention it before, but I'm with the Government."

Smithy sipped his coffee, allowing himself to make a face. Bloom smiled a little. "Was that for me or the coffee?"

"Coffee, mostly, though it's true I'm not what you'd call a fan of the boys in DC. So, they sent you up here, I take it? I guess that's better than if it were your idea. I'd hate to tell you the kinds of people that have sought me out."

"You used to be a Government man yourself, the way I hear it."

Smithy stared into the coffee mug as he swirled its contents around. "I guess they would have told you that. We took the Government's money, that's closer to the truth. We were a 'specially-retained task force,' and if you got one of our keepers to tell you more than that, you must have a lot more charm than I do."

Bloom carefully removed an iPhone from his shirt pocket and called up an app. "Task Force 'E'," he read from the screen. "Mind if I ask what the 'E' stands for?"

Smithy shrugged. "That was Wizard's idea, back when we were told there was going to *be* a Task Force. They didn't care what we called ourselves. The 'E' was for the Hebrew letter *hei*, I think, and for…Eris? The old goddess of Chaos. Wizard thought that was appropriate." Smithy shrugged again. "Never knew what he was going on about half the time. He read a lot, so I just took his word for most of it."

"Wizard," Bloom said thoughtfully, glancing down at his phone. "That's Lucian Evermore?"

"Unless he's no longer with us, and if you told me he wasn't, I'd say check your sources. Old Lucian's always been pretty quick on his feet."

"Dr. Albrecht Graham, called 'Brick.'"

Smithy smiled, and his eyes seemed to come close to twinkling. "You ever get to meet him you'll see why we called him that. Jingo always said we should've just called him 'Shithouse' and split the difference."

"Jingo, that's Jesus Maldonado?"

"Right. We started out calling him Sniffer, but he never liked that name. Always said, '*I don't sniff*!' like you were calling him a dog. Anyway, Brick suggested Bloodhound, but he didn't like that much better, as you might imagine. Wizard was going through his what-do-you-call…those books give you other words for things? Synonyms?"

"Thesaurus?"

Smithy smiled. "That wouldn't have been a bad name for Wizard, actually. But then we would've had *two* fights on our hands. Anyway, he was reading off other names for 'hound' and then 'hawk.' Jingo came up as a synonym for hawk as in 'warmonger.' Jess liked that one a whole lot better and it was getting late, so…"

"And you, Nathaniel Smith. Code-named Smithy."

"They were already calling me that when we first met, in the Corps. Just a natural nickname, I guess. And Brick said it was a good name for somebody always making things, like I was. I was always making little things out of paper, wire, wood, whatever I could find. Always liked keeping my hands busy."

Bloom turned to the bookshelf and pointed at a small wooden figure standing beside a stack of Faulkner novels. "Like that?"

Didn't see him looking around when we came in, Smithy thought. *This one's fast and quiet. Gotta keep an eye on him.* He got up and strode to the bookshelf, handed Bloom the carving. It was obviously supposed to be one of the Old People; there was a softness to the shape Bloom seemed to like.

"Nice craftsmanship," he said, rubbing it with his thumb. "Not too often you'll see something like this done from life. One of your friends out there model for it?"

"The big male that brought you here? Broken Tusk, I call him. That carving there is supposed to be his mate. I named her Anji." Smithy grinned. "I always did have an eye for the ladies. Anyway, I'm not a real blacksmith, but I do have that habit of cobbling things together. So that's where *my* name came from."

"I believe there was one more," Bloom said, setting the carving down and consulting his phone again. "A fifth…"

The smile that had been playing around Smithy's face dissolved. "That was Cap. Accent on *was*. He's the reason we're not taking the Government's money anymore. The reason I'm here and the others are…wherever they are."

"But you're all still involved with cryptids, in one form or another. I won't go into details about the paths your colleagues' careers have taken, but I imagine you know a little, anyway…"

Smithy sat down. "I do know a little," he admitted, reseating himself, "And since you know so much about me and my friends, maybe you'd turn the spotlight on yourself a minute. Like exactly what part of the Government you're with. They ain't all created equal, you know."

Bloom rolled his eyes. "Don't I ever. I worked with a unit back east that was involved in a disinformation campaign of sorts. I was writing books, giving lectures, all basically promoting the idea that Bigfoot and all the other creepy-crawlies were just so much fantasy and misidentified bears. At that point the boys in DC thought that was the best way to go. Since then, I got involved in a little kerfuffle over in western Pennsylvania, partially involving your 'Old People.' They were going to retire me early, I think, but at the last minute they asked me to broker this little meeting of the minds we're having right now."

"Lucky you."

Bloom fished a metal card out of his pocket and handed it to Smithy, who narrowed his eyes at it.

"Jacob Stone?"

"Ever heard of him?"

"Don't get many society papers up here, I'm afraid."

"Multi-billionaire. One of the really big boys the bloggers and news shows don't talk about. If you put together everything he owns or has a piece of, you'd be looking at a medium-sized country. That card in your hand is incredibly valuable. A tacit invitation to meet with him. There's not a businessman in the world wouldn't chop mommy's head off to get one of those. In his entire career, he's only given out six. Two of the original recipients are now deceased, as of a decade ago. You and your friends are the remaining four."

Smithy leaned back in his chair, stretching his long legs out on the wooden floor. When he spoke, his drawl had grown more pronounced. "Well, shoot, what's he want with us? I'm just an old Carolina boy barely finished his last meal of smothered squirrel. The others aren't much higher up on the food chain." He didn't take his eyes off the card, which he rubbed gently with his thumbs.

Bloom took a deep breath and began talking. Smithy didn't take his eyes off the card as he listened. When Bloom finished, he took another swallow of cold coffee. Smithy waited till he set the mug down, then took it and strode over to his stove. He pulled open the small door and began shoving pieces of firewood in.

"Might as well get another pot going, if you're agreeable. Sounds like you and me got a lot to talk about, Mr. Bloom."

THREE

A call woke Rhiannon from a deep sleep. She checked her phone and sighed. Half past four in the AM. Still, it could have been worse. Her first night at New Eden, the calls had started right after she got her boots off and hadn't ended till around ten the next morning.

She could hear Aaron's heavy breathing as soon as she picked up.

"It's the dogs, Rhi. They're going crazy." There was an angry, blaming whine in his voice. Typical Aaron. He was scared, and Rhi didn't exactly blame him. The "dogs" he was talking about weren't dogs, as such. Not the four-legged kind.

"Where are you?" she asked calmly, settling herself on the edge of her bunk and reaching for the vial of caffeine tabs she kept handy on her night table.

"Where do you *think* I am?" he asked testily. "I'm in the Box in North Four I was on patrol. Just getting ready to wrap it up. Next thing I know the whole damned pack jumps out of the trees and comes running for me." A muffled crashing noise came from the phone, followed by a gasping snarl.

"Dammit," Aaron muttered. "When can you get out here, Rhi? I need backup bad!"

"Roger that," Rhiannon said, taking a moment to tip a couple of tablets into her mouth. She quickly chased them with the dregs of a cup of lukewarm water she had left on the table. Breakfast of Champions.

"I'll be out as soon as I can. Can you get Getz? He's on North Two tonight."

She knew perfectly well Aaron had called Getz before reaching out to her. The only reason he had called her at all was because Stone had insisted she be involved in every kerfuffle that came up—and they came up pretty regularly up here. And if Aaron hadn't called Getz, she would have. She wasn't freezing her tits off in central Alaska so she could play Stone's cute little pet grad student while he put her in life-threatening situations on the daily.

Aaron scoffed. "He's on the way, *supposedly*."

Rhiannon hoped Getz had gotten more of a briefing than Aaron's usual histrionics. The German was strong and more than capable, but he'd better be packing firepower. If he'd gotten the idea Aaron's whining amounted to no more than a single grumpy crypt, and he went in unarmed…well, it wouldn't be good.

"Okay, sit tight and don't take any chances. You know the protocol. I'll be out asap." She hung up before he could start snarking again. *Swear to God, that man will go to his grave bitching.*

She got geared up and climbed onto the sled waiting outside her quarters. Stone had commissioned the sleds from a Belgian firm when planning for New Eden was in its earliest stages.

The vehicles were low and sleek, like a cross between a bobsled and snowmobile. They were fast and so easy to manuever, Rhi's little old granny out in Scottsdale could drive one. Using the trails that linked the reservation's four quadrants, they could get you from North Four to South Four in what felt like an eyeblink.

Rhiannon glanced up at the starry skies as her sled shot down the trail. It reminded her how much she loved it out here, even though working for Stone was more often than not a pain in the ass, and dangerous to boot. But there was none of the crap you had to deal with in the cities, no pollution, no crowding, no lunatics laying for you in the shadows. She'd been thrilled when Stone had offered her the job. It had involved taking time off from her Ph.D., and of course she had signed documents promising to keep her mouth shut about the real purpose of New Eden, at least for the time being.

That meant losing contact with her family as well. She hadn't been crazy about that, and she knew her family was probably going crazy by now, her father in particular. Rhi had a pretty good idea what he would say about his brilliant daughter working with a monster.

And his pets.

When the reflectors posted on the trail switched from red to blue, signaling she had switched over from Central to North, she slowed the sled down. The Box Aaron had called from was one of many sprinkling the reservation, sturdy cabins with heavy insulated walls, kept well-stocked with provisions and weapons, just in case things ever got out of hand some fine night. Normally they were protected by ultrasound shields, but Rhi wasn't getting the sickish feeling in her gut that ultrasound normally produced. Not too surprising; even Stone balked at the cost of keeping the shields on 24/7. Powering that kind of tech was expensive.

Approaching the Box, Rhiannon could see tall dark figures moving restlessly around it. They ran crouched over on back-bent legs, their heads muzzled and topped with what looked like horns or spikes, which Rhi knew were really ears.

Yup. Dogmen.

One of the difficulties with working with the cryptids of any kind was that so little was known about their biology and metabolisms, let alone their psychology. Stone didn't like *medication* of any kind—one reason, ironically, that he himself was in his current state—so even if they knew what cocktail of drugs would knock the dogs out, he wasn't likely to authorize their use. They had rifles for cases of, as Stone called it, absolute necessity. The arsenals also contained specialized arms whose workings had never been explained to Rhi in terms she could understand. They were apparently effective for subduing larger creatures, but there weren't a lot of the devices on hand, and Stone preferred they be used exclusively in the field. Especially in places where glimpses of them could be counted on to scare or impress the locals.

One type of weapon, though, she had become very familiar with: the wands. She took hers from her belt, putting her thumb on the power switch and keeping it there. The wands were ultrasound devices that sent any cryptid hungry or angry enough to take a bite of you running. Rhi had an idea her father would love to get his hands on Stone's ultrasound devices, and he wouldn't be using it for subduing 'squatches. Plenty of rich countries would pay big money for that kind of tech. It worked fine on poor countries too.

So, Rhiannon and her colleagues were stuck with the wands and the occasional rifle for when things got really hairy, and what little they could suss out about which training methods worked— on dogmen as opposed to 'squatches, lake wyrms, reptoids, and all the rest.

She ducked down behind some shrubs, carefully watching the dogs as they continued their restless circuit of the Box. Now and then, one would launch itself at the Box's walls for a moment, clawing mindlessly at the walls while uttering short, ugly howls. There was no telling what had set them off. They might have just been hungry for live meat, instead of the bloody chunks of freshly-slaughtered deer and moose they were typically fed. Or maybe they just didn't like Aaron—that certainly wasn't impossible.

"Rhi!" A hoarse voice was calling to her from behind a nearby tree, beckoning to her with a gloved hand. Squinting, Rhiannon could make out Getz's bulky figure peering owlishly at her. He was a powerful figure in padded black body-armor, his round face fringed with a short beard. The rifle he cradled in his arms added to the threat. He was easily the largest man on the staff, but his thick-lensed glasses gave him an oddly scholarly appearance.

"Be careful, Rhi," he told her in his hoarsely-accented voice. "Something's wrong."

"Ya think?" Rhiannon muttered, moving carefully to join him. She saw his point, though. Despite their wolflike appearance, dogmen were not really pack creatures; in the Midwest, where they'd been most commonly sighted, they were rarely spotted in groups, or even pairs. They were without question dangerous, but if it came to a choice between attacking a human or making themselves scarce, they would pick the latter option every time. Stone was convinced that they, like all cryptids, had some kind of purpose, and their solitary natures were somehow part of that.

But now it looked as if all the dogmen in New Eden had gathered together for the single purpose of trapping Aaron in his Box and giving him a heart attack.

"So, what's our plan?" Rhi whispered. Protocol dictated problems be met with as few staff members as possible; Stone probably would have frowned at a two-person back-up, so summoning Corben or Simone wasn't really an option. Of course, protocol also laid down that harming any of New Eden's cryptids in any way was an absolute last resort. So, they couldn't simply open fire on the dogs and hope for the best.

Next time I get a one-on-one with Stone, I should talk to him about scaling back protocol a little.

"I think we have two options," Getz said. *"Der erste,* we leave Aaron in the Box and stand guard here to ensure the *hunde* don't get inside with him. By morning, maybe they will leave on their own."

"Possible." It certainly had the advantage of being a cautious approach. Stone would like that.

"Der zweite, we can take the offensive and try to either frighten them off, or lead them far enough away for the other to get inside, get Aaron, and get him away by sled." Not a bad plan under the circumstances, but far more dangerous.

Rhi's phone rang at that moment, making both of them wince. She always put it on maximum volume before bed, and in her hurry to get to the Box, had forgotten to turn it down. She didn't have to check it to know it was Aaron. Worse, the dogs had heard it. The entire group turned glaring at them, their ears first pricking then folding flat onto their narrow skulls. Then they were coming, snarling and foaming.

"Guess Aaron just picked for us," she said, aiming her wand. "Cover me, but try not to kill all of them. Stone will have our heads."

"Wait, let me try something." Suddenly Getz was loping off to the right. He fired his rifle into the air, then started off again, discharging another couple of rounds. The dogs heard the shots and angled off towards him like a flock of birds suddenly changing course mid-flight. "Get Aaron!" he yelled.

Rhi didn't waste time arguing. If the dogs got hold of him, he was better equipped to live through the mauling they would try and give him. Still holding her wand at the ready, she ran as fast as she could towards the Box, raising her phone to her mouth and answering Aaron's call. Luckily, he hadn't yet hung up.

"I'm coming!" she said. "Get out here and stay beside me. My sled is just outside, on the right."

The Box's door slammed open and there was Aaron. He took just enough time to kick it shut and immediately fell into step beside her as she changed directions back to the sled. Aaron was about her age, with close-cropped blonde hair and a pinkish complexion. When she first came to New Eden, she'd found him sort of cute. These days, not so much, though now she appreciated how fast he could run.

One thing that puzzled Rhi was the knapsack he had slung over one arm. The rifle he clutched was one thing, but what the hell was he carrying? That sack looked heavy. She spared him a quick, quizzical look as they got on the sled, but he looked past her. Suddenly he didn't seem as scared as he had been just moments before. It was as if they were off for a joyride on a sunny day.

Weird.

She kickstarted the sled, looking nervously over her shoulder. The dogmen were converging on

Getz, backing him towards the Box. The big man kept them at bay with his rifle, jabbing the barrel at them with loud curses in German. The dogs knew what the rifles did; they had learned to be cautious when a human had one. But that didn't mean they were giving up the fight. They were watching him with shining red eyes, waiting for a chance to converge on him and take him down.

"Did you lock the door?"

Aaron blinked uncomprehendingly at her. "What?"

"The *door*," she shouted. Getz had electronic keys, like all the staff, but he might not have time to use them. If Getz could quickly get into the Box, he'd be alright, at least temporarily. He could call for backup while she was racing back to Central.

"I...I don't remember."

Rhi cursed in frustration. "Stay here," she said, climbing off the sled.

"What?" Aaron cried again, his fear returning in a rush. "You can't leave me here!"

"So, drive the sled back. You know how."

"But I..." Aaron was struggling to undo his safety belt and get to the driver's seat. For a moment Rhi struggled with an impulse to go back and help him, but she stifled it. Aaron had the same training as anyone on staff, after all. *He'll be alright.* She kept going towards the dogmen, unshouldering her rifle from its clip.

She fired a short pulse with the wand and the dogs turned, wincing and staring at the low hum.

The barely audible noise turned her stomach, but it was harder on the dogs; cryptids seemed to work at a different frequency than humans, which was fine with her.

"C'mon, puppies! You already had your biscuit tonight; time for bed!" She spoke loudly, aggressively, trying to mask the nervousness creeping over her, slowly curdling into outright fear. Most people had that reaction to cryptids, especially when they got a close look at them. It wasn't something that could be explained in natural terms. She had worked hard to suppress that unreasoning fear, knowing that if she didn't succeed, working for New Eden would be pointless.

The creatures began advancing on her, cautiously but clearly with malicious intent. Slaver dripped from their long jaws, their fangs glinting in the moonlight. They walked slightly hunched, their clawed hands reaching…and then, as one, they were charging her, moving with startling speed.

Rhi very nearly lost her nerve at that point. It would have been so easy to hunch down and cover her head, bawling like a child as she waited for the dogmen to take her. But she managed to get her wand up and fire it full blast at them. She gagged, and the dogs jerked back, pawing pitifully at their ears. But they were still coming, in some cases obviously forcing themselves to keep running.

Then, there was a loud *crack*, and a dogman in front jerked upright to its full height, crying out, and then falling heavily to the ground. She barely had time to register it before the rest of the dogmen had reached her—and ran right past her. She could smell them as they rushed by—the reek of unwashed fur mixed with *something*, that indefinable stench of ozone that so often accompanied cryptids, even lake wyrms.

Then it was gone. She caught a glimpse of Getz on his knee, his rifle carefully aimed. *Good aim, big man*, she thought, lifting a grateful hand. But then came another distraction: Aaron screaming.

Rhi turned and saw him on the ground, a trio of dogmen on top of him. The sled sat idling near him, the lights glowing. Poor bastard had just managed to turn on the ignition before they got to him. He was writhing in a pathetic attempt to get away from the claws and fangs savaging him. And he was holding something, Rhi saw. His knapsack. A dog had hold of it in his claws, and the two were engaged in an almost comic struggle for it. Aaron's determination to hold onto it was surprising, Rhi could see not just the gleam of blood on him, but clouds of steam rising in the frosty air. *Dear God, have they torn him open?* The pain should have incapacitated him, but he held on till he finally went limp. The dog tore the pack off him just as Getz managed to fire another shot. It started, then went running, the pack clutched to its chest. A moment later the others joined them. Moments later, the woods were silent. Even the sound of their running feet was gone.

Rhi ran to Aaron. The whole thing had happened so damned fast, before Getz could even get his rifle up. "He's dead?" Getz called, moving carefully around the dead dogman as if the thing might get up at any moment and jump him.

Rhi stopped short next to the steaming pile that had been Aaron. She turned her head, willing her stomach to calm down. "Yeah," she muttered. "He's dead." Something that combined the strength and natural weapons of a wolf and the vicious ingenuity of a human being could do a lot of damage. *Who'da thunk?*

Stone wouldn't like it, not because he was a compassionate soul who cared about his people— the idea nearly sent Rhi off on a laughing jag she knew wouldn't stop if she let it out. And it wasn't that he would be worried about the legal ramifications; he had fixers and lawyers like a dog had fleas. But dead workers set a bad precedent. The kind of people willing to work at places like New Eden—the *qualified* ones--weren't that easy to find, and they talked to each other, on a shadowy network that mainly functioned online. If word got out that one of Stone's pets had killed a worker--even if it was the worker's fault—it would give his little playground a bad name.

And he *really* wasn't going to like the dead dogman. The only time a cryptid had died at New Haven had been when a nameless thing from South America, not unlike a bipedal tapir, had simply dropped dead, presumably from the cold, though Stone had set it up in a hella expensive enclosure with heat and all the trimmings. Still, Rhi didn't think shooting the dogman would get herself or Getz fired, though she couldn't be sure.

Either way, it wasn't a great start to the week.

"Come on," she said, moving gingerly past Aaron's remains to the sled. "We have to report this. By the time we're done it'll be daylight. I'll buy you breakfast."

"Yes," Getz said, setting off to where his own sled was parked. As he passed Aaron he stopped suddenly and began poking at something on the ground with the barrel of his rifle. "What's this?"

Rhi looked over at him. Getz had stooped and was lifting something from the ground. It was hard to make out in the dark, but it looked like a gleaming chunk of glass, around the size of her fist. "What is that?"

Getz walked silently towards her, holding the thing out for her to see. It was a stone, but not the kind she had expected. It was a deep green, cut into facets that caught the moonlight. An emerald, probably worth a year of her salary, or likely more.

"Jesus," Rhi breathed. "Did that fall out of Aaron's backpack?"

"Must have," Getz said. "When the *hund* took it."

Rhi took the gem and turned it over in her hands. Where the hell had Aaron gotten a jewel like this out here? And, the question of the century: what the hell had the dogmen wanted with a whole backpack full of them?

FOUR

"You want another beer, Lucian?"

Lucian Evermore pushed his tattered golf-cap back on his forehead. "I'm okay for now, thank you, lady." He liked a little taste in the evening, but the discipline that had been part of his life for so long made it hard for him to enjoy much more than that, retirement or no retirement.

And he hadn't been feeling all that good today, honestly. It wasn't a sour stomach or sore head; something was nagging at the back of his mind, making him antsy. Worst part was, he knew that feeling from way back.

Denise smiled down at him, moving close enough that her thighs bumped him. She made a nice picture with the Florida sun setting behind her. *Not to mention that red bikini. I mean, damn.* "You like something a little sweet?" she purred.

"Nothing sweeter round here than you," Lucian smiled. He lifted a hand to stroke her leg.

"Lucian!" Denise's daughter Remy came running up from the houseboat's lower deck. She was carrying a softcover book that seemed larger than she was, running clumsily with it. "Lucian, I finished the book!"

Remy was a plump little girl; she hadn't inherited either her mother's leggy build or her looks. She sure wasn't going to make it in the pageants like Niecie had, but seeing her warmed

Lucian inside. *Not a good idea to get attached*, a voice inside him warned. He ignored it. *If that's the way I was built, I wouldn't be wearing my grampa's old fishing hat, like the high-hats wear their medals.*

"Girl, stop yellin' like that," Niecie scolded. "What I tell you about bothering Mr. Evermore when he's resting?"

Lucian silenced her with a frown, then turned back to the child. "Now that's what I like to hear!" he said, lifting an arm to welcome Remy in beside him. "You like it, baby?"

"Uh huh," Remy said, nodding till her braids flew about her head. "I liked the parts with the wizards." She looked at him. "Momma says you were a wizard, one time," she said.

Lucian cut his eyes at Niecie, glaring harder than he meant to. "Aw, that was just a nickname these friends of mine gave me one time."

"Were they good friends?"

Lucian smiled. "Well, we all fought like the devil half the time, but...truth? They were the best friends I ever had. I know lots of people don't have brothers like that, let alone friends. I hope you find friends that good one day."

"I bet you really are a wizard," Remy said softly, leaning close to him as she flipped through the book.

"Read me your favorite part," Lucian told her, settling back on the cushions. "Or even a part you don't like so much. Tell me *why* you didn't like it."

He could feel Denise smiling down at them. She was often short with the girl; she had come to motherhood early and patience wasn't high on her list of virtues. Lucian knew a big reason she had stayed so long was that he was so good with Remy. Since they'd moved onto the boat with him, the girl had stopped wetting the bed, and had finished the school year with more Bs than Cs. Not exactly scholarship material, but there was time yet. *So now you feel even more obligated to stay*, the voice in him murmured. *Wizard gonna be a daddy now? Awesome.*

"*Somebody*'s gotta make dinner," Niecie said, heading belowdeck. Lucian knew that meant "Somebody's gotta order the pizza." Fine with him. One night with extra pepperoni instead of fish and salad wasn't going to kill them. He watched her go, admiring the way her hips swung, then turned his attention back to Remy, who was working her way through a paragraph, sounding out the larger words one syllable at a time. Her awkwardness didn't matter; the book was well above her reading level, and she was comprehending it fine. When he was Remy's age, he'd started out with crappy Gold Key Comics and a year later something clicked and he was working his way through Gibbons' *Decline and Fall*. His family thought he was bewitched. Some things you just couldn't predict.

Lucian looked up at the sunny Florida sky. He should have been perfectly content, what with the setting sun and the sounds of his neighbors starting their nightly parties. But he was nowhere near content. That squirmy, uncomfortable feeling wouldn't let him rest. He tried hard to concentrate on Remy's reading, but it was like it used to be when he tried reading himself and that feeling came over him.

His eyes flicked around the marina, realizing he was looking for something. Expecting something. *Not again. Please God, that's all over.*

Monster's coming, the voice said, relentless.

Suddenly it was there, a towering pillar of pallid flesh shooting up out of the water like a goddamned cartoon beanstalk, the underside lined with a row of ugly saucers the size of dinner plates. Some of them looked chewed, half worn away. The pillar wavered for a minute, then fell heavily onto the deck, hard enough to make the boat rock.

How big is that mamma jamma? That ain't no octopus like the sushi chefs cut up for you...

Remy squealed, burying her face in his chest. Lucian wrapped his arms around her, holding her tight. While the main tentacle rolled around, a mass of smaller limbs boiled onto the deck, each one squirming manically, tearing at the boards with clawed tips, like a blind man feeling for something with his fingers. Its flesh changed color as he stared, going from that dead corpsey grey-white to pink, then flushing coral red and finally a deep, unhealthy orange. People on the marina's walkway had seen the thing and were gawping at it, all of them hauling out their cell-phones to take pictures, even though the light was getting dim. Lucian stared at the thing as wide-eyed as any of them, as though he didn't know perfectly well what it was.

Lusca, he thought dully. *Is that a fuggin' lusca?*

Then things got bad, and very quickly. Niecie came up onto the deck to see what the noise was about (or, knowing her, maybe to bitch because she couldn't put the pizza order in with all the ruckus going on). She cried out when she saw the thing, and even though Lucian was yelling at her to get back down, that he had Remy—she ran to them in a panic, unwilling to let anything happen to her child.

She was barefoot, and the water that had slopped over the polished boards of the deck made it slick. She fell onto her face and the lusca registered the vibration. Instantly, tentacles of varying lengths and widths were shooting over and around her.

Just like you'd expect a mutant octopus from hell to do.

Lucian disentangled himself from Remy, shushing her while he kept a desperate eye on her mother and stretched internal muscles he hadn't used in years. The lusca was sick; it was old, too, but something—pain or a discomfort similar to the one that had lately gripped Lucian—had driven it to the surface and onto the boat. It was out to get prey, and not just eat it, but strangle it, tear it limb from limb. Had that something been hoping

Lucian would fall into its clutches? Maybe, but it didn't matter; Niecie was the one it had caught.

Not today, Satan.

Lucian didn't keep weapons on the boat; even if he had a gun or a fishing spear, it wouldn't do more than momentarily inconvenience the lusca. So, the folding knife he kept in his pocket for odd tasks around the boat was as good as anything. He allowed himself enough time to get it out and open the blade, then ran for the lusca, kicking his flip-flops off as he tore across the deck.

They weren't killers, or hunters. Cap used to say that wasn't in their job description, nor in their blood. They had mental weapons, strong ones, but sometimes those weapons needed a little help.

The thing had Niecie wrapped tight in its multiple arms, looking more like a spider's breakfast than an octopus'. Lucian plunged the small knife into the main limb and, tightening his grip round the handle, dragged it down through the whitish meat. His senses were sharpening; there was no cry of pain from the thing; it had nothing to scream with. But he could feel the sharp bolt of agony going through it, opening it up on the inside. He used that opening.

Go. Get out of here. Go back down and kiss Davey Jones' ass. Nothing here for you, Satan. He kept his thoughts sharp and hot. The creature's response—a wordless blast of unreasoning pain--came to him so hard he nearly lost his balance. He kept on going, driving the blade deep into its flesh.

Thousand-Arms. Sea demon. Dagon's bitch. I didn't invite you up here, but I'm sure's hell showing you the door.

The sickness in the creature made it pitiful, as did its response to the cutting. Hurting it quickly became a hellish task. Lucian's stomach turned as he worked away at it, but soon enough it retracted its arms, reluctantly releasing Niecie onto the deck. She lay coughing for a moment, but by the last shake of her shoulders she was back on her feet and running towards Remy, snatching her up and sobbing.

Some of the smaller tentacles rose up and reached for Lucian, clawing at him feebly with the talons on their tips. Nothing consequential, but a few of them drew blood. He slammed a foot into the biggest limb, and that was enough, finally. The lusca began to withdraw, slowly sliding back over the deck and over the railing. He could hear the churning of the water as it went in.

He ran to the deck and got a glimpse of something vast and whitish and fringed with many arms, sinking into the darkness. In time it was gone. Lucian glanced up at the spectators. A few gave weak cheers. One kid gave him a thumbs-up, but their reactions were all strangely sluggish. Several women in bright beachside outfits were already walking away talking about where to have dinner. Two men traded comments on the photos their phones had captured, as though it were nothing more than some interesting species of fish.

They would never quite forget, but nothing would come of the incident. It would pass into local legend, that time the big octopus came out of the water on Key Benjamin and tried to attack a houseboat. The pictures and videos would filter down into the cryptozoology blogs, to be endlessly debated. Nobody from the larger world would take notice or believe any of the stories. *And it's just as well*, Lucas thought drily.

He turned to Niecie. Remy struggled free of her arms and ran to him, crying "Wizard! I told you you were a wizard for real!" Lucian winced a little, but didn't bother correcting her. *Looks like that's the direction we're going in*, he thought. *I'm Wizard again. Yippee skip.* He stooped down and hugged her, and when he pulled away after, he thought he could see something in her eyes. A little gleam, faint but fierce, that startled him. Wizards didn't kill monsters with folding-knives, but with spells. Had she heard some of the thoughts he was flinging at the lusca?

She *won't forget today*, he thought. *Is she gonna be one of the ones?* He hadn't ever even considered the possibility, much as he loved the child. But you never knew about these things.

Denise had already come to snatch Remy away from him. "Lucian, what was that thing?" she asked. Both she and her voice were shaking. Lucian couldn't blame her.

"Niecie," he said gently. "Remember I told you I had been involved in some strange things one time? Well, that was one of them."

"I thought you were joking!" she said, sounding not quite angry, but a long way from happy. "I thought you was playing with me!" Again, he couldn't blame her. By morning the incident would be faint in her mind, but it didn't matter; in a very basic way, her world had been turned upside down. It wouldn't ever be just Instagram and beauty pageants, and, *Girl, Arielle just got me a part in Doggie G's new video* anymore.

"Come on, baby," she said, dragging Remy away. "Let's go down to our cabin, get you cleaned up." The girl didn't cry, but her eyes never left Lucian's. He stood on the deck with slumped shoulders, slowly coming down off his adrenaline high. He shut his eyes and forced himself to breathe normally.

Denise would be leaving, and of course she'd take Remy with her. There'd be nothing acrimonious or accusing about it; they'd both be grown-ups. There would be talk about her visiting her mother up in Orlando and maybe looking at some new parts she was planning on trying out for, maybe something about a new school for Remy. But she would never come back to him, never even to visit. He would never see Remy again.

He stared down at the slime-smeared blade of his knife. *That's how these things go. It was a mistake to let her come here in the first place.* Sighing, he went to get the mop and begin the task of cleaning up the deck, before he could get to feeling sorry for himself.

"Mr. Evermore?"

Lucian turned and saw a man on the walkway, looking up at him. He wore a kind of armor of padded black nylon. The guy made a strange addition to the marina crowd of brightly-dressed tourists. He had a mild-looking face, but Lucian didn't doubt that when he meant business, you would know it.

"Are you Lucian Evermore, sir?"

Lucian frowned. "Far as I know. What can I do for you?"

The man motioned at the boat's gangplank. "Permission to come aboard?"

"Come on." Lucian stood waiting, wiping his knife on his shorts and folding it back into a pocket, watching the man closely. He wasn't expecting trouble, but then again he hadn't been expecting a full-grown lusca to nearly capsize his boat.

"Got a call for you," the man said, taking a small black phone out of his pocket. Burner phone, a throw-away. The next second, it was ringing.

Lucian could refuse to answer, and he doubted the man would try forcing him to the deck and pushing the phone into his face until he said hello. But he wanted to know what this was about. He took the phone and put it to his ear.

The line buzzed emptily for a moment, then a familiar voice said, "Wizard?"

Lucian's shoulders shook a little with silent laughter. *Man, I do believe this day just got a little bit better.*

"Hey, Smithy. How the hell are you, man?"

FIVE

Manuel's fiancé wanted a "destination" wedding, but besides any questions of having the money Manny was cheap as hell, so the "destination" was demoted to Mom's backyard in Oxnard. Manny wanted one of his buddies to do the ceremony, a moderately successful Youtuber named Eliphas Deathkiller. Eliphas had picked up a mail-order title declaring him an official reverend of the Church of the Holy Panjandrum, legally able to perform marriages. Ronnie nixed that fast; Manny was going to argue, but by then Mom had gotten word of it and that *really* killed it. Mom made a quick call to Father Purcell at Mary Mother of God, and that was that. Manny and Ronnie were having an actual-factual Catholic Wedding, even if it wasn't going to be held in a church.

Marriage, Jess had always heard, was all about compromise. That seemed about right, though Manny seemed inclined to sulk.

Jess got to the house early so he could tune his guitar. Mrs. Rivera down the street was catering and her sons were already out in back setting up tables and hauling in huge boxes of frozen *lumpia*. One of the Rivera boys was tagged to tend the open bar. He was sweating in his monkey-suit, arranging the plastic glasses in pyramid-shaped towers. He tossed Jess a cold beer to keep him company while he teased *skreeks* and *skrawwks* from his old Stratocaster.

Jess sighed and looked up at thin clouds drifting over the white California sun. He felt old. Not because at fifty-two he was playing punk-rock guitar at his younger brother's wedding, not even because that was all he could afford to give him. Maybe because so much of his adult life had been spent fighting monsters and, despite his partial relief at having escaped that, he still felt a certain malaise. Squaring off against mothmen and giant Komodo dragons wasn't exactly fun, but nothing after had ever quite measured up.

He had returned home to his family after the team broke up. Like the others, he had been left with a substantial pile of shut-up money from the government, but most of that had gone to buy Mom and his younger sibs a new house and set up Manny in a business that had, over time, failed. The house, at least, looked better than ever. Jess himself had spent most of his time bumming around the coast, returning home to play dollar beer nights in local bars, and helping out Manny in his business, sometimes just packing orders in boxes for days on end. He'd grown his hair long and steadfastly resisted Mom's attempts to set him up with this or that nice girl in town. When she asked him why, he'd just said, "Well, you never know what's lurking around the corner." What he didn't say was, sometimes the lurker had claws and big teeth.

Jess didn't like to admit it, but sometimes, out in the park or fishing McGrath Lake, he would get a little twinge. He'd lift his head and inhale the breeze, with its hints of smog and oil, and every now and then a really good whiff would come to him over all the citified stinks. That's why the guys had tried calling him "Sniffer," much to his displeasure.

These moments seldom lasted very long; pretty soon he'd wonder if he'd really smelled anything at all and get on over to the grocery store to pick up soy sauce for Mom or head down to Charles' to have a beer with Arnie. But once...*one* time, and right near the house, the scent hadn't backed down immediately. He'd got a glimpse then of something hiding behind a dumpster in an alley, something with claws and scales and glowing red eyes. He was pretty sure it was female, and, though he couldn't have said why, pretty sure it hated him like poison.

Then it was gone, taking its scent with it. If it hadn't been for that moment, he might have started forgetting in earnest. Just another Oxnard bum.

But he hadn't. Not quite.

"Hey bro, you wanna give me a hand with this?" Jess looked up to see Manny struggling to carry a good-sized keg through the back gate. He had Mom's gift of masking what he was really thinking, but in a way that made it plain for anyone to see. What he was thinking now was, *you gonna stand around all day messing with that guitar while everybody else does the work?*

Jess set down his guitar and went over to help. Funny Manny should get an attitude about others shirking; he'd never done anything else in his life. *Guess that's why he wears fancy suits when he doesn't have a dime. Why he drives a beamer when he still lives at home and lets mMom cook him breakfast every morning.*

"Manny, this is the first time I saw you lift a finger all day, so quit being a jerk." Ronnie was standing in the back doorway, glaring. Jess grinned. He liked Ronnie; white girl, nice build, red hair that was dyed red like roses, not like what they called ginger. She had a tat on her left shoulder, kanji for "TRANQUILITY," which was a hoot, because Ronnie had a mouth on her. She had strong opinions, like the idea that the groom shouldn't see the bride before the wedding was nonsense, or, as she put it, "horse-puckey." Jess wasn't the only one in the family to think she'd keep Manny in line.

Ronnie watched the brothers bring the keg in, setting it up by the free bar. The Rivera tending gave them a thumbs-up, then set to work tapping it.

"You guys go get changed!" Ronnie said. "I swear to God," she fretted. "Father Purcell isn't even here yet and we're supposed to do this at two!"

"Yeah, two o'clock, but that's not Pinoy Time," Jess grinned.

"S'right, babe," Manny laughed. The reference to "Pinoy Time," was the closest he came to wearing his Filippino heritage on his sleeve. "That's not how we roll in the islands."

Ronnie cast an imploring look skyward. "Whatever! Just go change, please. Manny, I think Antonio's here. *He's* already got his tux on!"

As he followed Manny into the house, Jess caught a glimpse of his cousin Darna at the kitchen table in her best party dress, struggling to make artificial roses out of crepe paper and wire. Darna was a little hyper—Jess suspected she might be a bit on the neurodivergent side, though he knew his sister would freak if he were to mention it. She had suggested the roses as a way to keep the girl busy until go-time. Darna wasn't having a good time of it, though. She couldn't get the rose formed to her liking, and finally slammed the crepe down and sat with her arms folded, scowling.

"You go on," Jess told Manny, seating himself across from Darna. "I only have to put on my suit." *Seeing as how you picked Antonio Bautista to be your best man.* If Antonio hadn't grown up right alongside the Maldonados, Mom wouldn't have stood for it. Jess didn't really care; he hated tuxedos.

"Hey, what's goin' on?" he asked Darna, helping himself to crepe and wire.

"I'm not real good at this," Darna said sadly. At twelve, she was long-legged and clumsy, but you could see the beauty she would grow into. "I suck at it."

"Yeah?" Jess smiled. "Well, I'm not good at anything." *Except maybe fighting mapinguary and Mongolian death-worms.* "Let's suck at it together, what do you say?"

They spent the next half-hour working on roses together chatting about Darna's school. Mom ran in and out, stressing about whether there would be enough food. She and Mrs. Rivera were old friends; she knew damned well there'd be enough *pancit* and *adobo* for a small army, but Mom wasn't used to having a party she didn't do all the cooking for. Ronnie's bridesmaids were already upstairs, fixing their makeup while sisters did their hair, complaining about tight shoes, gossiping about who was dating who, cheating on who, dreaming after who.

"You know that big cat Mrs. Aquino had?" Darna asked suddenly. "The grey one?"

"I think so," Jess said, frowning at the straggly pseudo-rose his efforts had turned out.

"Well," Darna said, leaning across the table with an air of someone about to share a great secret. "He's *dead.*"

Jess blinked. "That's too bad," he said. "What happened, he get run over?"

"No," Darna said, her eyes glowing. "Something *killed* him. Mrs. Aquino said she found him in her back yard, and he was like a papier-mâché cat, like a *pinata.* She said he was like all sucked dry. No blood. Even his *eyes* were all dried out."

Suddenly Jess' stomach burned with anxious fear. "When was this?" he asked.

"Just this week! Poor Samson! I heard Mrs. Aquino telling Mama he had two holes in his neck, like a *vampire* got him!"

"Yeah," Jess muttered. "Honey, you okay for a minute? I have to run outside and see if Father Purcell is here yet."

"Sure," Darna said, gesturing at the roses. "I think we have enough, don't you?"

But Jess was already out the back door.

***

He caught the scent the minute he opened the door. It didn't exactly knock him over, but it was far too strong to be ignored. Except ignoring it was what everyone out back was doing, their minds occupied with their pre-wedding tasks.

Jess took the three steps down to the ground in one jump, forcing himself to not just take off running. His brother Diego gave him a mildly surprised look, then went back to setting plastic cutlery beside the plates set out on the folding table.

"Who're you, dude, the Six Million Dollar Man?"

"I'll be right back," Jess said, making for the gate.

"You could give me a hand out here, when you come back. I heard Father Purcell's on his way."

Jess nodded absently, already setting off down the street, eyes flicking into every yard he passed, under every porch and car. Every time he thought the scent was dying away, he'd twitch his nose and it came back to him three times stronger. Wherever it was, it was coming in his direction.

Fine with me, beastie, he thought, heart pounding. *Just stay away from the wedding, kay? From my fam.*

His family was blissfully unaware of what he'd been doing with the team. To them, cryptids were just something you saw in cheap docu-shows on the History Channel. All they knew was the laziest kid in the Maldonado clan had finally found a decent job, and after twelve years he'd come back home flush with that good Government money. Better that way. Much better.

Something flashed by him on his right, accompanied by a blast of that smell; a little musky, a little like old meat. Too fast for him to get a good look, but as he whirled to face the way he'd come, he caught the slightest glimpse of something low and squat rounding the corner, the faintest *click-click* of claws scrabbling on concrete.

He ran. A year and more of Mom's cooking had him out of shape, but he wasn't yet working on a gut, like Manny. The raw-throated screams erupting from back in the Maldonados' yard pushed him on, adrenaline burning inside him.

Something had climbed onto the gate and sat crouching with its back to him. It was big as a good-sized boxer, with a brownish-grey, pebbled hide that moved slowly with its breathing. A row of spines ran down its back, to the base of a whiplike tail that slashed slowly like a metronome from left to right as it considered its prey in the yard beyond. Its head was lowered between its high shoulders. Someone in the yard yelled above the general cries of fear, "That's an *aswang*, man! Like my *lola* used to talk about!"

But it wasn't an *aswang*, Jess knew. You heard funny stories from the old country that seemed too credible for comfort, but the *aswang*, by and large, was a creature of folklore. This was something else entirely, a cryptid that had taken up residence in the day-to-day world.

Chupacabras. Not one of the mange-eaten coyotes that had somehow acquired the name in the press, but the real deal: a reptilian monstrosity ugly as sin, more than ready to suck on anything, not just goats. Cats like poor Samson, for instance. There had been mutterings from the research-boys about them penetrating California up from Texas, but at the time Jess hadn't thought much about it; he and the team had enough on their hands at the time.

"Goat-sucker!" Jess yelled, trying desperately to get its attention. *If it gets in the yard, it's gonna start killing.* "Blood-drinker!" It didn't turn. The human pickings in the yard were a lot more appealing than the skinny Flip yelling at it. Jess' searching eyes found a discarded beer bottle on the ground, and a good-sized stone. He snatched up the latter and flung it at the thing's back. It bounced off its spine, doing no real harm, but serving to catch its attention.

By then Jess had caught the bottle by the neck and gave it a solid knock against the fence post. He put force behind the blow, remembering Cap saying *This ain't the movies; stuff doesn't just break on its own so you can look all macho.* It shattered, leaving him with a serviceable blade of sharp glass.

By then the chupacabras had turned to look at him, and Jess inhaled sharply. He had forgotten how ugly the damned things were.

"Diego!" he yelled, keeping his eyes on the creature's. "Get everybody inside *now*!"

"Jess?" Diego's voice called, breathy with disbelief—not so much about the monster invading their yard but the new note of hard authority in his brother's voice.

"Just *go*, man!" Then Jess mentally pushed his family away and raised the broken bottle, fixing eyes on the chupacabras, willing it to return his gaze.

The thing's head was human-like but barely, with mismatched onyx eyes that seemed like blobs of oil smeared onto its reptilian skin. Its lips hung loosely from a complicated arrangement of fangs that put Jess in mind of an insect's mandibles. He'd seen chupacabras' mouths in action before, the inner jaws stretching to attach themselves to a sheep or dog's while the lips moved to cover them and ensure all the blood went where it was most wanted. And the noise they made during the exsanguination process…he thought of the chupa getting hold of Manny or Ronnie and had to stifle a gag.

The creature seemed to hear his disgust; its lips retracted a little, showing what might have been a grin.

"Come on," Jess breathed. It would be a close battle, but it was only one; he felt sure he could kill the monster, or at least incapacitate it. Afterwards, he could worry about what he'd tell his family, while they figured out if they wanted to go ahead with the wedding.

Then things started going to hell. Someone yelled and then Manny was tearing up the yard running at the gate, clutching one of Mom's kitchen brooms like a ball bat. He was still half-dressed, in socks and shirt-sleeves, but his eyes were burning, hepped up on adrenaline.

"Fuckin' *diyablo*! Fuck you!"

"Christ, Manny, *no*!" But Manny was on a mission. The broom connected solidly with the chupacabra's head, knocking it off balance onto the ground. It thrashed around, shrilling and clawing up clots of earth. Then it flung itself on top of Manny, its weight forcing him down, pinning his shoulders with clawed hands while its mouth opened and made an awful keening sound.

Now others were barreling out of the yard, Maldonados and Riveras of both sexes, and a couple of heavy-set white boys Jess knew were Ronnie's brothers. They carried whatever they could pick up that looked like it might hurt a monster: carving knives and scissors from the kitchen, another broom, a mop, hammers and mallets from the utility drawer.

"Get away from it!" Jess yelled, frustrated. He knew if he could just slip his blade of glass into it, he could lay it flat. He could see himself doing it. *For Christ's sake, leave it alone, it'll kill you*! But the wedding party seemed to be doing alright, slamming into the chupacabra again and again until it could barely stand. It squealed, trying frantically to get enough purchase on the ground to spring.

Then it seemed to leap into the air, only to jerk suddenly, venting a loud shriek that went through Jess like a knife. It fell back to earth with a thump and lay twitching.

Something shot it, Jess thought dully. He wasn't ungrateful, but his neighborhood had always been peaceful. The idea of Mrs. Aquino or David Nguyen not just packing but using their weapons against a chupacabra didn't exactly calm him.

Manny ran up and caught him up in a bone-cracking hug, followed quickly by Ronnie and several more of his sibs and cousins. For a moment he felt good—really good. He saw Darna on the outskirts of the crowd, smiling and clumsily wiping away tears.

"Mr. Maldonado?" A van had pulled up on the street behind him. It wasn't the kind of vehicle people drove here in the hood. It was big and sleek, with black windows. Several men in padded black armor—who could only have come out of it—stood around watching the crowd dispassionately. Two more were coming with what looked like a plastic body-bag and, quickly and efficiently, began bundling up the dead chupacabra. The wedding party moved back, watching them respectfully. Jess was a little surprised none of the fam had laid claim to it. He could just see it stuffed and mounted in Diego's living room.

"Jesus Maldonado?" the man asked, glancing curiously at several of the male partiers, as if he might have gotten the wrong guy.

"That's me," Jess said. He didn't like these guys' looks, but they might be a blessing in disguise; nobody would doubt they were some kind of Government team in charge of wayward monsters, freeing him of the necessity of awkward explanation.

"Call for you," the man said, smiling in a way Jess wasn't sure he liked. He held out a small flip-phone, the kind pushers used. "You're welcome to take it in the van, if you want some privacy."

"I'm just fine right here," Jess said. He already had a pretty good idea who was on the other line. He put the phone to his ear and took a deep breath. "Hey, Smithy," he said.

SIX

If Stone's voice had been just a bit less human, Rhi thought, it might have come as a relief. You could just imagine him as a robot, or as a man in a wheelchair with some kind of speech aid sticking out of his throat. The fact that he insisted on taking meetings through an audio conferencing device, so that you couldn't actually *see* him would have aided in the illusion.

As it was, the voice emerging from the device on the table was clipped, mechanical...but full of little tics and uncertain tangential mumblings. Also more than a few wet smackings and slurps that suggested a man who couldn't quite control his lips.

But it couldn't have been that. As Rhi understood it, Stone didn't *have* lips.

"Howh-h many dogmen died?"

Rhi forced herself to sit up straighter in her chair. "Just the one, sir." *Like I told you five times already*.

"Mrmph. And."

"And Aaron, yes," Getz put in calmly. Corben and Nakamura were at the table as well, along with Vaughn and Patel, all of them expressionless, looking like they were putting on a show of attention while willing themselves to be somewhere else. There were a lot of other staff at New Eden. They were attending to various afternoon duties; supervising feedings, checking on recent acquisitions, setting up exhibits in "the museum," and a goodly number of other tasks. Stone liked to have as many people as possible at meetings, but they couldn't *all* be there, though he'd tried to arrange it a few times early on. Rhi suspected he didn't want to lose the opportunity to deliver an object lesson, should penalties need to be meted out.

"We still don't understand what happened to set the dogs off," Rhi said. "As far as we can tell, they just randomly attacked Aaron while he was on patrol. He's never had trouble with them before. None of us have."

"And we don't know what Aaron…you know, what he was doing with the jewel we found." Getz gestured a little at the emerald, gleaming on the table in the scanty afternoon light.

Stone made a long, low sound that gradually rose in pitch, until it became a whistling gurgle. It sounded as though he were either in considerable pain, or simply couldn't control the noise. Either way, it didn't make for pleasant listening. Rhi squirmed in her chair; even Vaughn and Nakamura, who were normally so self-controlled as to seem barely human, looked disturbed. Getz shut his eyes.

Other sounds came from the device; calm voices and the sounds of furniture being moved, along with a number of unidentifiable noises. Stone's nurses, probably, administering medication or some other form of care. Stone's gurgling call of distress gradually lowered in pitch, becoming more rhythmic. Rhi realized he was singing—or something like it. A hymn...it sounded like "A Mighty Fortress is Our God."

Some of Stone's nurses seemed to be singing along with him, or at least humming. This kind of participation was always encouraged; Stone seemed to find it calming when his people joined him with the hymns and sermons and "Amens." The nurses tended to be most accommodating, not unnaturally; since they spent the most time in his company, they had a stronger motivation to keep him happy.

Finally, the singing trailed off and Stone said, "Give Thierry the jewel. Then you all may-yehh return to your duties...but consider yourselves on a first demerit."

"Yes, sir," Rhi said glumly. Not a great meeting, all in all. She had been expecting Stone to demand all sorts of data—the times of death, any available autopsy findings—and at least some speculation on where Aaron had gotten the emerald and why the dogs might have wanted it. But whatever episode had overtaken Stone had pretty much deep-sixed any deeper discussion. She wasn't really disappointed to avoid the extra work, but she was left feeling oddly frustrated and out of sorts. A man had died, after all, though not a man who was particularly well-liked.

The direction to hand the emerald over to Stone's personal assistant was a far more onerous punishment than the demerit. Granted, the demerit wasn't exactly good news; two more and they might be looking at termination, but Rhi would gladly have taken five extra demerits over having to speak to Thierry.

Getz swiped the gem off the table and pocketed it, giving Rhi a questioning look. "Shall we get it over?"

"Might as well." Their colleagues were already making for the door, Patel giving them a sympathetic look. She and Getz followed them, Rhi reflecting as she went.

One wall of the hallway they walked through was all glass; an enormous window that overlooked the rugged terrain of New Eden. A broad swath of grass stretched down to the beginnings of the Northern Forest. The afternoon was shaping up bleak and overcast; nothing about the scene made Rhi want to do anything but go back to bed. But she was scheduled to feed the lake wyrms in East 2. *Just as well,* she thought. *I couldn't sleep right now if I tried.*

Still, she lingered behind, staring through the glass. There were no signs of any cryptids anywhere. No 'squatches lurking at the first trees of the forest, no dogmen running hunched across the grass, nothing prehistoric-looking flying against the grey skies. They were all off in their separate environments, doing whatever it was they did by daylight. *They're as hard to spot up here as they are down south.*

Not for the first time, she wondered what she was really doing up here. The thought of working with creatures thought to be mythic, growing human understanding of them, and eventually introducing them to the wider world was intoxicating. It fit in well with her degrees in Biology and her minors in anthropology and folklore. But in the time she'd been here, the reservation had, if anything, become more insular. Stone, already far stranger than her expectations, had grown still weirder.

And now people were dying. Would Aaron be the last?

"Rhiannon?" Getz' voice broke her out of her gloom. She nodded and set off towards where the big man stood at the end of the hall, waiting for her.

I'll give it one more year. But after that…

Away from the window, she didn't see the bulky dark figures emerging, moving towards the House. They stood in a knot just outside the glass, watching her form move down the hallway. Then, slowly, they began to disperse, moving back into the trees but not disappearing entirely.

And the day went on…

PART TWO

SEVEN – WASHINGTON, DC

The four men each entered the conference room from a different door, flanked by blank-faced security guards. Three had flown into Dulles from their various destinations, the fourth into Reagan National; all were badly jetlagged, but they gave no sign of it as they rolled into the room. They all seemed jittery with suppressed energy; it was hard not to notice the way they avoided looking at each other. They strolled around the room, touching the chairs around the table, or rapping on the table itself, as though for good luck or to test how sturdy it was.

One, a young-looking Filipino man with a long black ponytail and a straggly Fu Manchu mustache, headed straight over to a table covered with refreshments and began heaping a plastic plate with pastries.

"Man, Uncle Sam hasn't gotten any more generous," he remarked, eyeing the scanty number of Danishes.

A lean black man in a vest jacket, a fishing cap seated on his head, strolled over with his hands in his pockets, a lopsided grin on his face. "Man, you better watch that kind of talk in this place. They might call your mama on you, spank that long butt of yours."

The Filipino man lifted a finger to forestall the conversation while shoving a pastry into his mouth. Then he made a series of herky-jerky martial arts moves, much to the other's amusement. "You talkin' about my mama? Huh? I'll spank *your* butt!"

The other two men approached each other slowly, grinning. One was even taller and lankier than the black man, his sandy hair so unevenly cut it was obvious he had done the job himself.

"Dr. Albrecht," he nodded. The other man was powerfully-built, with tanned, muscled forearms and a broken nose. His red hair was short and curly, and the wire-rimmed glasses he wore looked absurdly delicate on his heavy face.

"Dr. Albrecht?" the man said, making a show of looking around him. "I don't see no Dr. Albrecht. I see...lunch!" He ran at the other, nearly knocking him off his feet. The two wrestled standing, both bellowing with laughter.

In a moment all four were laughing and embracing each other, slapping backs and throwing mock punches.

Like teenagers, Marty Bloom thought, entering the room last. Recent research had it that Faculty X might, among other effects, suppress aging to a limited degree. *Sure looks that way*, he thought, a little glumly as he watched the reunion. Maldonado was probably the youngest, but even he was in his early fifties. Marty was well past fifty himself, but he both looked it and—most days—felt it. The Task Force apparently didn't.

"Gentlemen," he said, clapping his hands softly. "Listen, I don't want to be a wet blanket. I appreciate that you haven't seen each other in some time." *But the brass don't like jollies. They've already canceled Christmas.*

"But we've got a lot to cover. General Flynn will be here in just a few…"

The four men stopped roughhousing, breathing hard and seemingly making. Smithy, the one he knew best, said, "We know the general, Marty."

"That's right. We took marching orders from him for a *while*," Maldonado said, kicking at the carpet with a frown, as though curious whether his foot could succeed in removing a section.

Dr. Albrecht—Brick--sauntered over to the refreshment table and poured himself a Styrofoam cup of coffee. "And he knows *us*," he said wryly.

"That's the damn truth," Wizard muttered, taking a seat at the table and diving into one of the briefing folders that had been laid at each table. When he looked up, he was frowning, but his voice had softened somewhat. "And he doesn't much like us. Mr. Bloom, I'll remind you of what we all made clear to your people. We ain't none of us *agreed* to anything here."

"That's right," Brick said, sipping at his coffee. "There's been no commitment of any kind."

Maldonado nodded. "And if the good General says there was, we reserve the right to disagree."

The rear door—the one Smithy entered through—opened and a large, bald man in an olive uniform entered the room, followed by several men in suits. His chest was heavily laden with medals.

"Disagree about what, Lieutenant Maldonado?" the man said in icy tones. If he thought he was intimidating Jingo, he was mistaken.

"Well, for one thing," Maldonado drawled, selecting another pastry, "the fact that I'm no longer a lieutenant, or possess a rank of any kind."

"Not speaking for anybody, but I'm pretty sure that goes for the rest of us too," Wizard grunted, not looking up from his folder. "I *know* it goes for me."

"And me," Smithy said. Brick nodded, frowning, making his own opinion on the subject clear. One of Flynn's underlings, clearly seething, opened his mouth to protest, but Smithy simply spoke over him. "No rank, no affiliation of any kind with any military, U.S. or abroad. We sorted all that out when we left. We all know your views on that, sir. Afraid they don't much matter in this case.

"Now, General, if you don't mind, why don't we get down to business? We all came a long way for this—some of us longer than others," he added, motioning at Brick.

Bloom watched the exchange with interest. It was the first time he'd seen anyone not just stand up to General Uriah Flynn, but simply disregard him, as though he weren't particularly important. He'd already decided he liked Smithy; he was rapidly coming round to the others.

"If you don't have any objection, General, I'll kick us off," Bloom said quickly, walking to the front of the room. The Task Force members sat down willingly enough, stretching their legs out as though they were in a movie theater instead of a briefing room.

Bloom picked up a remote from the table and the words NEW EDEN appeared on the far wall. "Each of you have been separately contacted by a man named Jacob Stone. He's a very wealthy individual, as I've explained to Mr. Smith here. Makes the usual names look very small indeed. He's known to big players in the business world, but not many others, partially because he shuns publicity, and takes certain steps to ensure he stays out of the limelight. And there are other factors as well."

"Not to interrupt, Mr. Bloom," Wizard said, "but I've done a little homework on Mr. Stone— I'll agree he's not an easy man to get information on. But on that 'other factors' business--there are some very peculiar rumors about him. He's a long way from your average reclusive multi-millionaire."

"Correct," Bloom agreed. "For one thing, he's got a particular interest in cryptids." He clicked the remote again and the screen changed to an image of a wooded, mountainous area. What looked like clip art of a sasquatch, a reptilian-looking creature and a plesiosaur-like creature had been copied awkwardly in. Though the plesiosaur was obviously aquatic, it had been placed awkwardly on a patch of green grass, with no water in sight.

"Nice artwork," Jingo commented, prompting new scowls from Flynn and his flunkies.

"A quick job from one of our interns," Bloom said smoothly. "It was meant to illustrate our understanding of Stone's 'New Eden' project. Round about fifteen years ago, he bought a large parcel of land in central Alaska. Very hush-hush. Naturally we were interested, but it took our people a year to learn anything beyond the fact that Stone acquired the property. We knew there was a considerable amount of building going on up there, but our reconnaissance teams couldn't get near it."

Jingo rubbed a thoughtful finger over his scanty mustache. "Why didn't you just invite yourselves in? I mean, Alaska's part of America, last time I looked. And you're the government, after all." He cast a nasty grin at Flynn. "They can't say no to *you.*"

"Lieu...*Mr*. Maldonado, I..."

Bloom jumped in quickly. "It was considered essential we maintain a low profile. We could have confronted Stone directly, yes. But since he was being so secretive, we wanted to be careful. There was no telling what he was doing. At first, we were thinking human trafficking, cash laundering, all the usual suspicions. We wasted a lot of time, a lot of taxpayers' dollars. Then we lucked out. One of Stone's people came to *us*. He was in dire financial straits, desperately needed money. He came to us with this."

Another *click*, and the screen showed something that caused sharp intakes of breath from Flynn's men, but barely any reaction at all from the Task Force members. Bloom turned his head slightly, so he wouldn't have to look at it.

The image showed a mustached man with a drawn, nervous face, standing next to a dead creature of some kind, hung on a hook on the side of a shed. The man looked like a fisherman posing next to a prize catch, but whatever kind of creature the corpse had been, it was no fish. It was man-sized and covered in what appeared to be short, ashy fur. Wide, pleated appendages grew from its back and shoulders and wrapped around its trunk, hiding it. They gave the impression not so much of folded wings as of an umbrella's furled canopy. The shoulders were broad, and completely headless.

"Moth," Wizard said coolly. "Not just any cryptid—baby mkole-mbembe, frozen snowman— this is a damn Category Three. See how it seems to change when you look at it, even when it's projected on a wall?"

That was true. It was a big part of why Bloom didn't like looking at it, why Flynn's men squinted, muttering profanities under their breath, trying to process what they were seeing. Because the mothman wasn't *always* headless; in the blink of an eye, it seemed as though the body were crowned with a misshapen head and a weird face, half insectile, half anthropoidal. Sometimes the face was crowned with curling, feathery antennae, sometimes not. Then, another blink and the head would be gone again, and red eyes like bike reflectors would be gleaming from the hairy shoulders.

Most disturbingly of all, in some of the iterations it was suddenly the man beside the creature who was suddenly missing his head, his body resting limp against the wall and streaming with blood. Thankfully, there weren't many of those.

Silence reigned over the table for a time as the men studied the creature.

"You all know I don't go in for this 'categories' business," Flynn said. "'Plural realities' and all that." One of the younger security men smirked in agreement, as though a string in the back of his head had been pulled.

"Either it's an animal or it's not," Flynn went on, "even if it's extraterrestrial in origin."

Brick spared the General a mild grin, as though what he'd just said was an old but not particularly good joke. Then he returned his attention to the screen, as if Flynn were no longer present.

"So, what happened to the moth?" Wizard asked sharply. "And maybe more to the point, to the dude who brought it to you?"

"The informant was paid off," Bloom said, "and sent on his way."

"I'll bet he was," Jingo said cheerfully.

"The subject there—the 'moth,' as you call it— was put into storage after a thorough examination."

"Which I'm guessing turned out inconclusive," Brick drawled.

"Central Alaska is some rough territory," Smithy broke in. He was no longer looking at the screen but at a large paperclip his long fingers were busily unfolding. "Inhospitable, you might say. If Stone wanted to stay remote, that's not exactly a bombshell. But it's a funny place to start a cryptid farm. If Stone's got Category Twos on his wish list along with the Old People and some surviving pteranodons, he's castin' his nets pretty far. Why not some nice remote island in the North Atlantic? Just as cold and miserable, a little harder to escape."

"I'd guess he's a little overconfident," Brick put in. "That's a problem a lot of these guys have. I did a little research on him myself. His family has roots in Alaska. That would be enough to convince him to bypass your island idea, Smithy. And I have a feeling this has something to do with it." He pulled a slim paperback book from his jacket pocket. "This was published a few years back. It doesn't list an author as such, but 'Jacob Stone' is credited as copyright holder in the front matter."

He handed the book to Wizard, who looked like he was champing at the bit to get a look at it.

"Now, where'd you get that?" Smithy asked. "I'd wager it sure as heck ain't listed on Amazon."

"I got a guy I keep in touch with," Brick said modestly. "Can find you most any book you got a hankering to read. Did some digging for me, found this copy in a little hole-in-the-wall in Buenos Aires."

"Shee-it," Wizard said, flipping through the book. "Your boy's with Universal Life."

"Correct," Bloom said quickly, noting the impatient looks on Flynn and his people. "That's ultimately why he's begun New Eden, his 'cryptid farm,' as you put it."

"Check this out," Wizard hooted. "This book has a whole chapter on cryptids. Says they're all Nephilim, the degenerate offspring of angels and human beings. They call them *Homo nephilensis*, even though half of 'em don't look anything like people."

"So they're not just talking about the Old People?" Smithy asked. "When the hoo-has start going off on '*Nephilim*,' that's usually what they mean."

"If I'm readin' this right, they mean *all* of 'em," Wizard said grimly. "Old People, dogmen, wyrms, oceanic monsters, merfolk, they don't differentiate. They think *all* cryptids are abominations before God."

"Heck, if old Stoney's a Universal Lifer, there's no need to worry," Jingo shrugged. "Just mail him a copy of some of the stuff the Atheist types are puttin' out. His head will explode."

"If half of what I dug up on him is true," Wizard said, "we wouldn't even have to wait that long. Man's in bad shape," he said, shaking his head. "In all kinds of ways."

"Why *are* you worried about him?" Smithy asked Bloom. "I've never been able to figure out whether you crowd even believe in cryptids half the time, despite all the evidence."

Flynn was looking close to apoplectic. "Mr. Smith, we do *not* need to explain our…"

"If you want our help, you will," Wizard drawled, still paging through the book. "Or at least you'll give it the ol' college try. Otherwise…shoot, I've got a date with some half-smokes down at Ben's. I can leave now just as soon as later, if any of the boys want to join me."

"Dude, I never met a chili dog I didn't like," Jingo said, trading fist-bumps with his colleague.

"There is an issue that puts this higher on our priorities," Bloom said, aiming his control. The unsettling image of the dead mothman was suddenly replaced by a photo of an attractive young woman with auburn hair and intense green eyes.

"Her name is Rhiannon Merriman," Bloom said.

"As in *Senator* Merriman?" Brick asked.

Bloom nodded. "Correct. She just got her Ph.D. in Anthropology from Harvard. She disappeared soon after. She's in New Eden, presumably working for Stone. We're assuming he has her under an ironclad NDA, but we know she sneaks occasional calls to her mother. Those calls were traced to Central Alaska."

"Alright, so…?" Brick asked.

"The Senator is very worried about his daughter—understandable, since he and Stone were acquainted at some point. He's sent people to try and get her out, but…"

"If Stone's that powerful, guess they didn't get very far."

Bloom made a wry expression. "That's one way of putting it. I have a feeling they were lucky to make it home alive."

"We *know* Stone has Rhiannon Merriman in New Eden," Flynn said, obviously feeling the need to remind the room of his presence. "He seems to be interested in getting your help as well, gentlemen, undoubtedly because…"

"Because we possess Faculty X," Smithy said.

"That's right." The tall man's accusatory tone rolled right off the General's back. "So far as he knows, there's no connection between you and Rhiannon."

"You want us to go up to New Eden to meet with him and try to get Rhiannon back," Wizard said. "Keep your old pal Senator Merriman happy. But what you really want," he went on, narrowing his eyes, "is for us to get you the dirt on what Stone's doing, what he wants to do with his pet cryptids. Even if you don't believe in Categorization."

"That's right," Flynn said, settling back in his chair. "And we don't propose to wait forever for your answer…"

"You'll wait," Brick said coolly. "For as long as we tell you to. I'm thinking we'll have an answer for you by, say, ten tonight. In the meantime," he said, turning to smile at Wizard, "I think someone mentioned the word 'chili.'"

"Make you feel any better, General," Smithy said, "We can have one of your folks along to make sure we don't do anything naughty. You up for some half-smokes, Mr. Bloom? Maybe as good a bowl of red as they make this side of the Potomac? The boys and me here have kind of a tradition of hitting Ben's when we're in town and seeing who can eat the most of…well, anything on the menu, really."

Bloom glanced at Flynn, who looked ready to explode. "Off the record?" he said, inhaling. A wide smile broke his face open. "I'll bury you boys."

EIGHT

The back room in the House which served as Edmund Thierry's quarters and workspace reminded Rhiannon of nothing so much as a colossal greenhouse, with condensation-glazed glass walls whose thickness she assumed to be for something more than heat conservation. Here Stone's assistant spent whatever time left over from his other duties working on his true passion: cryptobotany.

The greenhouse's contents represented only a fraction of New Eden's work; cryptobotany was Thierry's obsession, not Stone's, but the older man was willing to give his majordomo some wiggle room to pursue his private interests. Thierry had been hired as an administrator, but over time managed to move up considerably. The few times Stone had directly brought up Thierry in Rhi's presence, it had been in the company of words like "brilliant" and "genius." Spending much of her adult life in various graduate programs had left Rhi with a healthy skepticism about "geniuses," but there wasn't much doubt the Frenchman was one of a kind.

Rhi and Getz moved slowly into the greenhouse, coughing a little at the mingled floral scents that filled the air, already perspiring under a blanket of intense, humid heat. Underlying these was a pervasive reek of decay, so strong it was difficult to tell if it were from vegetation or meat. The plants that filled the greenhouse ranged from pocket-sized succulents and oddly-shaped fungi to an actual tree, nearly twenty feet tall with strangely curving limbs that put Rhi in mind of the kraken in the Central Lake. She gave it a wide berth, whereas Getz gave it a quick, idle kick in passing. The tree's limbs immediately went into flailing spasms, proving the resemblance she saw to a kraken was no idle fancy.

"I will thank you, Mr. Getz, not to tease my subjects," a voice said. Thierry appeared from behind the tree, frowning with his hands thrust in the pockets of his lab coat. He was slender, with dark blonde hair pulled back in a dangling ponytail and round glasses whose lenses were heavily marked with thumbprints. Despite his slovenly habits of dress, Rhi had always found him remarkably handsome, with that indefinable air of sophistication many Europeans had. But within a month of their first meeting, she was thoroughly over him. Thierry was seldom actually unpleasant and never unprofessional, but he had a way of looking at you that made you think he was comparing you to his favorite specimen of *Dionaea muscipula*, and finding you distinctly on the losing end of the spectrum.

"Most of these plants are from tropical regions," Thierry went on, touching the tree's scaly trunk as though to comfort it. "Cultivating them here in Alaska has posed some very difficult challenges. They are used to far more temperate climates. We already lost the *upas*, as you know."

Rhi glanced at Getz. The *upas* was a tree in Thierry's collection that, technically, shouldn't have been considered a botanical cryptid at all. It wasn't the subject of travelers' tales or scientific reports, at least not for the last three hundred years. It was rumored to be so intensely toxic that—according to certain old stories—even a bird flying over it was subject to a sudden, painful death. The specimen in Thierry's greenhouse, kept completely separated from all the others, had apparently not been doing well. Rhi hadn't realized it had actually died. All questions of preferring animals over plants aside, that wouldn't have pleased Stone.

"Mr. Stone asked us to turn this over to you," Rhi said briskly. As if by prearranged signal, Getz removed Aaron's emerald from his pocket, offering it to the botanist.

"Mr. Aaron was attacked by the dogmen in the northern quadrant. They killed him. This jewel was found on him, and we believe he had a number of others the dogmen took."

"Ah, yes," Thierry sighed, accepting the jewel from Getz and tucking it in his pocket. "I heard. A bad business, no? Still, our efforts are not without risks. Aaron knew this even as we did." His voice was cool, though not excessively so. He sounded as though he were reeling off a speech he had spent weeks practicing.

"We're a little unsure what he was doing with jewels, though," Rhi said, "let alone why the dogs would want them so badly they would attack Aaron to get them." She watched the botanist carefully, looking for any sign her words had some impact. But Thierry only shook his head, looking a little irritated.

"I was not at all well-acquainted with Mr. Aaron," Theirry said, seeming to understand Rhi's probing glance. "I agree it is a puzzling situation; he did not seem a man to have secrets or be inclined to steal. But for anything further, I'm afraid you must look elsewhere. I will see this is properly investigated."

Meaning you'll hand it over to your winged monkeys and that'll be the end of it, Rhi thought irritably.

"Now if you will excuse me." With that, Thierry disappeared behind a stand of odd, reedy-looking plants.

"Charming as always," Getz murmured. "Shall we return to our duties?"

"Sure," Rhi sighed. "You know Stone will be asking him what time we handed over the gem, and what time we left." Sneaking a beer at the commissary, in other words, would not be a good idea right now.

"I'll need to get to South," Getz said, "but I'll walk you out to the sleds. Just let me use the WC." The big man was already moving back towards the door they had entered through.

Shouldn't have had so much coffee, Rhi thought wryly.

She sauntered after him, looking idly at the plants as she walked. The majority of them were carnivorous in one form or another; meat-eating plants were by no means unheard of in the non-cryptobotanical world, of course, but the majority of them met their dietary needs with houseflies. Most of Thierry's collection could take on anything upward the size of a small dog. Many had blossoms that were quite beautiful, but the majority had something a little strange about them, a peculiarity of shape that somehow made her uneasy. It was stupid, she knew; cryptids of any sort might legitimately be called monsters, but they were basically natural creatures, even though they suggested complexities to basic evolutionary theory. The dogmen were no more monstrous or even ugly than a timber wolf, the 'squatches no more so than a mountain gorilla.

Weren't they?

A sudden impulse made her turn from the door and move past a stack of boxes towards an adjacent room Thierry and the few assistants allotted him used as storage. There was a door in the room, she remembered, that opened directly onto a loading area. The heat and smells of the greenhouse were getting to Rhi. A short walk in the cooler air while she waited for Getz to return would do her good.

The sudden decision to move towards the exit in all likelihood saved her life. Something whistled past her cheek, with such force she jerked her head back with a loud cry of dismay. Whatever it was buried itself halfway into the wall with a loud *thunk*.

Instinct made her jump behind the back room's door, pulling it open in front of her to serve as a shield. More of the small objects immediately hit it, some bouncing off the glass panes, some piercing the wood and sticking there. Rhi squatted briefly, snatching up one of the fallen missiles before another rain of them hit. The thing was clearly organic; it gave the impression of a seed pod, sleek and wickedly pointed on both ends. She slipped it into her pocket, carefully scanning the greenhouse.

There were no signs of anyone concealed among the plants. The only movement was from a tall bush covered with hibiscus-like red blooms. Its fronds were moving with a slow, steady rhythm, reminding her oddly of the movements of a sea anemone. Rhi managed to snag a long dowel on the floor, probably used to steady young plants. When she waved it in the air, the blossoms seemed to contract, then abruptly expanded with loud puffs of expelled air. Rhi ducked just in time to avoid a fresh hail of darts, most of which hit the door and fell clattering to the floor.

Had the bush been there before? Try as she might, she couldn't remember. It was in a pot, so it could easily have been set in place while her back was turned…if that were the case, someone was out to get her, and the person who sprang most forcibly to mind was Thierry.

Rhi reached for her phone, but even small motion was enough to set the blooms twitching again. She risked a glance over her shoulder and saw the door to the loading area, gauging the time it would take her to get to it. The door she was crouching behind should still serve as a shield, and eventually the plant would run out of ammunition, but she didn't care to be too free with her chances. It was bad enough she might find the rear door locked. Inhaling deeply, she ran, keeping herself stooped over.

Much to her relief, the door opened under her hand. She moved quickly out onto the loading area…then stopped, staring.

The area before her was filled with 'squatches—some were the smaller varieties, red-furred and only as big as good-sized chimps. But most of the crowd was composed of really big ones, the smallest of them towering over her at eight feet at least. Luckily, she was standing downwind of them, but she still caught a whiff of the stench that even smaller specimens were known for.

With their slouched shoulders, the 'squatches gave the impression of waiting for someone or something—and from the sudden startled looks in their tiny red eyes, it wasn't her. Like most of the cryptids, they tended to avoid the area around the House. Also, like most of their brethren, they didn't tend to be dangerous—but given their size, it wasn't a chance she felt like taking. She lifted her phone to her ear and gasped when one of the largest of the creatures stepped forward and slapped it from her hand.

"Hey!" Rhi said, summoning as much force as she could. Her voice and manner might have scared off an uppity eight-year-old but even a small 'squatch was a very different proposition. She knew her wand would be a better deterrent, but close as the creatures were standing, she knew it would quickly meet the same fate as her phone. Her wrist was still tingling from the force of the blow. She was stepping backward at the same time, hoping to manuever back into the greenhouse. As an adversary, the dart-plant was beginning to look better and better.

Suddenly her feet left the ground. One of the big males had snatched her up, slinging her over his shoulder. The others were snarling at him, snorting through wide nostrils. Rhi had the crazy impression they were offering him advice on how to best carry the uppity female human. The male didn't seem to care. He began striding quickly, moving towards the forest behind the House.

Rhi's arm was crushed between her body and the male's shoulder. She tried to get a hand to her wand, but she was at too awkward an angle. What was worse was the way the 'squatch's reek was making her gag. She was forced to keep her mind focused on controlling her stomach. She didn't think the male would take kindly to her being sick down his back.

She could see the House dwindling behind her as she was carried away. The other 'squatches were following at a respectful distance, their eyes fixed on hers.

Rhi tried to think. Why was she being taken this way? There had long been lurid stories of male 'squatches carrying off human women for breeding purposes; she remembered doing a paper on that very subject, laughing through every page. It didn't seem so funny now. But she didn't think she was in any danger of being assaulted. The creature's manner was not amorous but urgent and grimly focused.

Night would be falling soon. Whatever the 'squatches' intention, she would soon be somewhere very cold and very dark, with no way of calling the House. Her only hope would be to wait till she was set down, then use her wand to get away. She knew this part of Central reasonably well. With luck she'd be able to get to a Box and phone for help from there.

Of course, there would be an awful lot of 'squatches to face down, wand or no wand.

Maybe I should have just gone into politics, like Dad wanted.

***

"Rhi? Are you still in here?"

Getz strode back into the greenhouse, frowning as he looked around. There was no sign of his colleague. She had probably decided to go on alone; perhaps one of the others had phoned her for help with something. Even so, something about the room struck him as odd; there was a strange energy lingering in the air, as if it had just been the scene of intense activity.

The back door that led to the loading area was ajar; several spiky things protruding from the surface caught Getz's eye and he moved towards it to investigate. The things reminded him in shape of a bird of paradise flower's unopened bud, wrapped in petals that gradually shifted from white to the palest green. They were half-buried in the wood of the door and it took Getz some effort to dislodge one for inspection. He remembered something he'd seen once, mentioned in a documentary on "extreme weather;" apparently during severe hurricanes a length of straw could be sent flying with enough force to pierce a telephone pole. Getz had been vaguely impressed at the time; now, turning the pod round in his fingers, he was actually startled. There were no hurricanes in Thierry's greenhouse. So, what had done this?

Then there was a hissing sound just behind him, and a sudden flare of hot pain burst in his lower back. Getz yelped and grabbed at the hurting spot. Another pod had lodged itself in his flesh, like a ninja throwing-star.

"You're looking for Rhi? You won't find her here."

Thierry had appeared from behind one of his plants, walking purposefully towards him. "She chose to go outside, I'm afraid. And there some of M'sieur Stone's pets took her. They are unlikely to hurt her," the Frenchman went on, his mouth twitching petulantly. "Which likely means I'll need to go hunting later. Or someone will. I do have work to do."

Getz's mouth moved. He was trying to speak, but no sounds were coming out of him. Thierry's fingers grasped the seed-pod and wrenched it out. Then he did make a sound, a gasp of pain.

"No need to thank me, I assure you." Thierry lifted his head and said something loudly in French, directing the words towards the back of the greenhouse. A moment later a young man appeared. Like Thierry, he was dressed in a white lab coat, though his was so stained that calling it "white" was an overstatement. One of Thierry's assistants, probably, though Getz couldn't remember seeing him before. He had apparently been interrupted during a lunch-break; he carried a half-eaten sandwich in one hand, taking a bite out of it as he stared incuriously down at the German.

Please, help me, Getz thought frantically. The seed that had pierced his skin must have infected him with some kind of venom, a paralytic of some sort. His back was hunching and his arms were curling slowly towards his chest, but his body paid no attention to his orders to get up. *Please, call somebody.*

Thierry and his assistant traded remarks in surly French. Then, cramming the last of the sandwich into his mouth, the younger man quickly dusted off his hands and got them under Getz's arms. Thierry took his feet, and the two moved towards the rear of the greenhouse, grunting and occasionally muttering to each other. Getz had very little French, but he made out one or two remarks: *eats too many dumplings*, was one.

Getz stared at branches moving past overhead, as well as trunks covered with moss and vines covered with blossoms. After a moment, something not quite in his field of vision twitched, like it was moving of its own volition.

Oh God, no…

They dumped him at the foot of the tree he'd kicked earlier. Thierry looked down at him, tight-lipped. "You understand, it's the easiest way," he said. "Not my idea at all. A bullet in the head would have been the route I'd chosen. Not completely painless, perhaps, but quick, at the very least. Expeditious. But Stone wants to avoid evidence that might be revealed later." The Frenchman sighed as the tree's branches began squirming down from above.

"It would have been better if you and your colleague had not found the jewel. Or if you had sold it and divided the proceeds with Rhiannon." One of the tree's tentacle branches quivered over Getz's leg as though smelling it.

No…

The tentacle curled round the German's ankle, then tightened. A moment later its grip was so tight it hurt. In another moment the pain intensified, turning to agony. At the height of it came a muffled but audible *snap*. Getz screamed wetly.

More tentacles were coming at him. The tips retracted, revealing branching claws that dug into Getz' flesh and pulled sharply back, tearing flesh away. The big man howled, then cried out as the tentacles worked their way under his back and tightened, hoisting him slowly into the air.

"*Alons-y*," Thierry grunted, signaling that his assistant should follow him. The young man said something in a distracted voice, keeping his eyes on the prone German, and Thierry shrugged. "*Putain pervers*," he chuckled, and kept walking.

The tentacles lifted Getz higher. Thierry's assistant grew smaller, staring up at him the whole time with dull, but eager eyes. At a height of about twelve feet over the floor, a vertical orifice opened in the tree's trunk. The wriggling limbs stuffed in the flesh they had torn from Getz's body, then came back for more. By the fifth time they returned, bone was showing through Getz's wounds, and his mind had retreated into somewhere more pleasant, a reservoir in his home town where he and his friends would go after school to throw stones in the water and speculate on which girls in their class might be open to selling their favors for pocket money.

He decided to stay there, where his body's cries of pain could be easily ignored.

NINE

The jeep pulled up to the edge of New Eden just before noon. Brick climbed slowly out, scanning the wall of evergreens before him, as though he expected at any moment for something to burst out and attack him.

"Anything?" he called to Jingo, who was sliding out of the back seat.

"It's Alaska, alright."

"Smartass. Any cryptids, I mean?"

Jingo joined Brick on the green, a duffel bag slung over his shoulder. "You need *me* to tell you this place is lousy with 'em? C'mon, Bwana Don." He gave Brick's safari hat a flick with his finger. "You ain't that old."

Brick gave him a lopsided smile. "It's bad, isn't it?"

"See above, baby. See above."

Most cryptids left their mark on the environment in far more subtle ways. At the moment those marks had Brick antsy as hell, as though the trees hid legions of dogmen and reptilians, silently watching their progress. He could tell Jingo was feeling the effects as well. He wasn't usually this obnoxious.

Then again, he hadn't seen him in years.

The jeep gunned its motors and turned slowly, its tires leaving ruts in the sopping ground. A moment later it was bumping back the way it had come, gradually picking up speed until it was no more than a spot in the distance. "Yeah, don't say goodbye, asshole," Jingo called after the driver.

Brick strode wordlessly up towards the green area that flanked the airport. They had arranged to arrive earlier than Smithy and Wizard, ostensibly to give them a chance to check out New Eden's western perimeters and any wide-roaming cryptids that might be present. Stone hadn't objected; or at least his people hadn't conveyed any objection. It was a relief not to have to come up with excuses to cover their real purpose.

Well, Stone knows who we are, and what we do. He may not know exactly why we're here, but that's his lookout.

Jingo lengthened his stride until the two were walking side by side. He had taken a banana from his pack and was methodically peeling it and breaking it up with his hands, shoving the chunks into his mouth. "We're getting close to the lake," he remarked, not looking at his companion.

Brick nodded. "Wyrms?"

Jingo swallowed and coughed loudly. "Like a hog's got ticks, man." He flung the banana peel into the trees. Announcing their presence. The direct approach could be dangerous, but pussy-footing around had its own risks.

Both of them were armed—hunting knives clipped to their belts, handguns thrust into their boots for easy access. The weapons were mainly for self-protection. They wanted to get a look at the local cryptids, gauge their condition and temperament, see how well Stone's people were caring for them. They couldn't get a game plan together without that. The local population of lake wyrms—any kind of water-dweller, really—would be a good place to start. They wouldn't be able to attack if Brick and Jingo didn't get a sudden urge to go swimming.

Scratch that...*shouldn't* be able to attack was more like it.

There was a rise ahead, hiding whatever was beyond. Brick and Jingo slowed their speed, faces registering caution. When they reached the crest, a large body of smooth water stretched out before them. They'd barely gotten a chance to scope out the lake before two long necks rose into view. Graceful as swans but vastly bigger. They were a good way out, but Brick could just make out the strange facial features—so blunt they might have been sculpted out of clay by an ambitious art student, but with weirdly mammalian features.

"Well, hello to you too," Brick murmured. Wyrms were notoriously shy, but these watched them curiously, seemingly in no hurry to dive again.

"Say hi to Auntie Nessie, you two," Jingo called, pulling out a cheapie disposable camera he had bought at the Fairbanks Airport. "Say '*Tullimonstrum gregarium, amigos*!'" He had no sooner aimed the camera than it made a loud grinding click that all but screamed *broke*.

"Listing pretty hard to Category Three," Brick noted, eyeing the camera in Jingo's hands.

"And how," Jingo said, holding up a long tangle of dislodged film for Brick's inspection. "Guy can't help but feel a little rejected." Like many cryptids, lake wyrms straddled all three Categories...physical creatures resembling species long dead, but with poorly understood ties to the realm of metaphysics and serendipity. The tendency of cameras to jam when it came time to photograph unidentified animals was by now almost a joke among the initiated. Aiming a camera at cryptids in the wild was thus a good way to determine Category, but Jingo's camera had done a lot more than jam; it had practically fallen to pieces in his hands.

"Okay, what's this, now? Brick said suddenly, gesturing at the lake. The wyrms were moving steadily towards the shore, their beady eyes fixed on the two men.

"Careful," Jingo said, taking a slow step backward. "They're coming like they mean business."

"No shit." The wyrms did not appear to be agitated, but their focus was unmistakable; it was the same focus Brick had seen in lions in Africa, ready to jump an antelope. "Get ready to run. No telling if they're going to try to come on land."

There was no telling, for that matter, if the creatures *could* leave the water. There were actually more than a few stories about supposed "lake monsters" appearing landside; even discounting those, the stereotypical conception of lake wyrms as jacked-up plesiosaurs rarely proved true in the wild. Still, most often they were purely aquatic…except, as with many Category Threes, when they weren't.

"C'mon man," Jingo said nervously, tapping Brick's shoulder, "let's beat feet. Get back in the trees. Even if they come out, they'll be too clumsy to dodge tree-trunks."

Brick nodded absently, fascinated in spite of himself. What Jingo was saying made sense, but he'd never seen anything like two wyrms actually approaching humans. He wondered if it had anything to do with their being in captivity. If they…

"*Crap!*" Jingo grabbed handfuls of Brick's shirt and yanked backward with all his strength, nearly pulling him off-balance but managing to get him out of the wyrms' range in the nick of time. Twenty feet from the pair, the cryptids suddenly dropped any pretense of composure and rushed the shore, roaring.

These still followed the basic design of a small head mounted on a long neck, ending in a heavily built, flippered body, not unlike an elephant seal's and maybe twice as large. Their heads were a lot uglier up close, club-shaped with tiny black eyes and gaping mouths lined with stubby but nasty looking teeth. *Bite your damned head off with those*, Brick thought.

In a second, he and Jingo were running down the rise towards the forest. Brick couldn't resist snatching a last look at the cryptids at the crest. They won't follow us, he told himself. If they try, they'll go ass over tea-kettle and that'll be all she wrote.

But, against all odds, and though their progress could indeed be charitably described as ass over tea-kettle, they *did* try.

The two wyrms came plunging and rolling down the slope, their bulk crushing young trees, their ridged flippers frantically digging at the earth for purchase, dislodging stones and causing small landslides of pebbles and dirt. They bellowed as they came, throaty roars with a whistling undercurrent. They sounded not just ferocious, but *angry*, somehow.

"Come on!" Jingo yelled, weaving between the trees. Brick headed after him. He glanced behind him at a creaking, cracking sound, and was amazed when the wyrms reared up to slam their bodies into the young birches in their path, handily flattening them.

"Jesus," Jingo said, eyes widening as he walked backward. He looked like a first-time tourist in New York, craning his neck to look at the skyscrapers. "Brick, *they know what they're doing*!"

The same conclusion had come to Brick; had the trees been more grown, with heavier trunks, the monsters might have had a more difficult time of it and eventually be forced to turn back to the water. As it was, they were able to use their weight to simply remove the obstacle the birches presented. Whether they considered the men prey or simply something they felt a strong urge to kill, they weren't going to let a few trees stop them. They might tire themselves out, but Brick didn't think so; he could sense a massive strength in those flabby bodies. If he and Jingo weren't able to get away, they'd be forced to defend themselves. A few bullets might slow them down, but Brick didn't like the idea. The team had agreed to avoid getting into any situations where they might have to hurt one of Stone's cryptids; they needed his trust, at least at the outset.

But where could they escape to? As Brick remembered, the forest surrounding the lake was fairly extensive. Now that they were in it, the maze of trees had trapped them every bit as effectively as they had thought to trap the wyrms. And it wasn't as though the forest might not be crawling with other dangerous cryptids; Brick couldn't sense any, but he'd learned that was no guarantee he wouldn't soon be feeling teeth clamping down on his leg.

They were trapped.

Unless they could find a hiding place…

"Look!" Jingo cried, pointing at a structure nestled among the trees ahead. It was a cubical, single-story building with one window on each wall, seemingly constructed of plain wooden sides. The briefing they had received from Flynn's people had mentioned buildings like this. Boxes, they were called. Supposedly they had been set up all over New Eden, providing bolt-holes for any of Stone's people who might suddenly need one.

Apparently, a constant wave of mild ultrasound was used to keep cryptids at bay, something that should serve to discourage the wyrms as well.

For all Brick knew, that might guarantee they were about to walk into a nest of reptoids. But right now, he was more than willing to take the chance.

"Hope the three bears ain't home," Jingo said, getting the door open.

"I'll settle for a bowl of porridge, and not getting my kidneys ruptured," Brick grunted, hurrying inside.

***

When the 'squatch finally set Rhi down, it was completely dark. She couldn't make out anything except the hulking shapes of her captors. The place smelled of evergreen—judging by that, and by the time she'd bounced on the big male's shoulder—they must be up in the eastern quadrant, where the forests were mostly spruce. East was probably the least populated quadrant, as far as cryptids were concerned. There were Boxes here, but not so many of them as there were in the other areas.

Rhi pulled herself to her feet, cracking her back with a low moan. *Next time remind me to take a taxi*, she thought. For the first half hour of her journey, she had planned to pull out her infrasound wand and send the 'squatches running; she had played the scene out in her head again and again, taking great satisfaction in every detail.

Now, hungry and thoroughly worn out, she didn't see the point. She could hear the 'squatches moving around her, chattering in their weird way that Stone categorically and inexplicably insisted was *not* a language, but so far none had made any threatening moves towards her. It seemed more essential to get a fire going to chase the night chill. The problem was, she couldn't see a damned thing. She had a small Firestarter in her pocket, but nothing to start a fire with. Her phone had a flashlight app that would have been useful, but thanks to Mr. Sasquatch that was back at the House.

Her best option was to grope on the ground, hoping her fingers would find a stick or branch that might make a serviceable torch. But everything her hands found—twigs and grass and last year's rotten leaves—were wet through. Just as her fumbling was growing frustrated, and she was starting to swear under her breath, something shuffled near her. Rhi looked up and saw a towering shape beside her, solemnly holding something long and angular towards her.

It was a branch, or part of one, and--thank God—it was more or less dry. She accepted the gift, assuming that's what it was, and dug in her pockets for her Firestarter and something to bind to her torch to be set aflame. A small first-aid kit—not much more than some bandages and a small vial of disinfectant—yielded enough gauze. There was some brandy—not high quality but very flammable--in the half-filled flask she carried in one pocket. And thank God again, she was anal about dental care—she had floss.

It took some time, but finally she had the torch sputtering in her hand. She took her time getting to her feet, keeping her eyes on the slowly growing flame as though daring it to go out. It was weak enough at first that she wasn't worrying about panicking her hosts, but once her eyes adjusted to the light, she saw she had other problems.

The hollow where she found herself was full of cryptids—and they weren't all 'squatches, though several varieties of those seemed to count for the majority. A group of dogmen stood hunched beneath a pine, tongues lolling as they took her in. There were a trio of crouching things with bulbous, staring eyes and scrawny limbs ending in bundles of grasping fingers. *Like that one thing...the Loveland Frog, they called it. Christ, I didn't know we even had any of those*! A few figures standing nearby might have been more frogs, or else garden variety reptoids. There were shuffling things she couldn't put a name to, and she could just make out a humanoid figure standing perched on a branch nearby, its features indistinct. All of them were facing her, watching.

The cryptids gathered around her all represented those types that were at least nominally Third Category; there were no relict species, no thylacines or ground sloths or dwarf sauropods and nothing that seemed like just another species of animal waiting to be classified. Most of these would have been classed as extraterrestrials back in the day. Rhi had experience with almost all of them in her time in New Eden, but now they were the ones with the upper hand—or paw, or claw or whatnot. Miles from her colleagues, with no way to call for backup, it wasn't a pleasant situation.

She felt her hand moving down to the wand clamped to her belt. Using it could be dangerous; these weren't trained bears. Whether or not they truly had anything like human intelligence, they might feel threatened by the ultrasound, and if they did, it wouldn't be pretty.

On the other hand, she very likely was going to need a weapon, and the wand was pretty much her only option. "Alright," she said, unholstering the device and holding it near the flame of her torch, so they could see it. "You know what this is? Just stay where you are. Stay back…stay…

"*Oh, shit!*"

As one, the cryptids began moving inexorably toward her. She flicked on the wand and the creatures stopped their tracks, baring their teeth and pulling their heads back as though something had them by the scruff of the necks. Rhi tried moving backward, but one of the frog-things shuffled forward and snatched the wand from her, making loud, belching noises as though to scold her. She wouldn't have been surprised if the thing had wagged a finger at her, like a disapproving aunt. *It might not be as affected by the ultrasound as the others*, she thought. *Hell, for all I know, it can dance the mambo.*

In any case, she was disarmed. But again, none of the creatures made a threatening move. Instead, they all began marching past her. The mothman-like apparition in the tree flew overhead. As they moved into the shadows, apparently unbothered by the lack of light, the frog, wand still in its paw, gave her a quick, sour-looking glance, as if to ask, *Well? Aren't you coming?*"

Sighing, Rhi began walking after them. At least she had her torch.

TEN

"I-hh must say, gentlemen, you'hhh haven't been p-particularly talkative," the voice from the microphone said.

"Well, Mr. Stone, it's not from lack of interest," Smithy said, leaning back in his chair. "That was a real interesting presentation you just talked us through…" *Lots more informative than what we got from General Flynn, I'll say that.* "It's just there's an awful lot to unpack there."

Stone made a grunting noise that might equally well have been agreement or impatience. Several of his people were standing with their backs to the wall, arms folded behind them. They looked more like soldiers than the combination of zookeeper, vet and animal trainers Flynn had led them to expect. There were two women among them, one Asian, one a sturdily-built blonde who looked like she'd done time working for Bond villains. Smithy was fairly sure neither of the two was Rhiannon Merriman.

"That's for damned sure," Wizard put in, sipping at his coffee. He and Smithy were seated at a table in a New Eden "conference center" that looked and felt a lot more like a millionaire's hunting lodge. A huge fireplace had been laid with blazing logs, any of which were easily as tall as Smithy, and the wood-panelled walls were lined with stuffed heads of various game animals:

Mountain goat, bear, various species of deer and wild boar. Smithy had been relieved there were no cryptids among them; no 'squatch, no mounted infant wyrms. That sounded like the sort of flex a man like Stone could be expected to indulge in, but there were apparently limits to his lack of taste.

Those limits, it turned out, didn't extend to the "museum" they had been walked through prior to the meeting. It took up an entire wing of the large building Stone's people called "the House" and contained enough nightmare-fuel for an entire generation. Because New Eden's collection, it appeared, wasn't limited merely to living cryptids. There were articulated skeletons of every kind of 'squatch Smithy had heard of or seen, mounted skins of everything from a zeuglodon to a rather scruffy little eohippus, all posed in highly realistic dioramas with accompanying plaques that read as if the text had been cribbed from Wikipedia. The pride of the collection was a massive baboon-like creature Smithy recognized as an African *chemosit*, with glassy red eyes. It looked as though it might at any moment awaken and jump out of its diorama to tear their throats out.

Seeing the creatures on display gave him a funny feeling, one he could tell Wizard shared. Cryptids had changed their lives, and they didn't always think fondly of them. But seeing them like this was…unsettling.

"Wasn't all that long ago you couldn't find anyone willing to even consider the existence of crypts," Wizard went on. "Not even the possibility they *might* be out there."

Smithy nodded in rueful agreement. *All those four-stars and high muckety-mucks would laugh at us so long's the press were around. Then they'd run off to the golf courses with their buddies, trying to figure out how the intel we'd given them could be used to line their pockets. And then when their plans went awry, they'd come right back to us, whining and begging for our help.*

"So, you'll need to forgive us if we seem a little close-mouthed," Wizard finished.

"B-but you *a-ahre* interested in my proposition," Stone said. Smithy resisted the urge to roll his eyes. Impatience was showing in his face, and Wizard stifled a cough with his fist. *Be cool, Smithy.* Smithy was cool.

His proposition was precisely what they'd expected. He'd heard of the Task Force's expertise. It was hardly public knowledge, but a man keeping his ears open could hear all kinds of things, especially when it came to esoteric matters like cryptids. He wanted them to work for him as consultants, part of his own unpublicized efforts to build a refuge, a sanctuary for cryptids, before—in time—revealing them to the world at large. The four of them would lend their knowledge of every form of cryptid to help New Eden's mission. Now that they were no longer officially tied to the US military, there was nothing preventing them from agreeing.

And the pay, of course, would be very reasonable.

Smithy didn't like the man's voice at all. It wasn't just his manner; Jacob Stone had that quality of assuming everyone in the world was dying to work for him...or to be his personal servant. They had encountered that plenty of times before. Nor was it about the mechanical sound of Stone's voice. But there was something odd about the tone and rhythms of his speech, the little stutters and slurs. Stone didn't sound like a man speaking through an electronic speech device; he sounded like an entirely different kind of creature altogether.

Every now and then certain types of Category Threes—mostly 'squatches-- would make some effort to "talk human." Something about the results could turn your hair white. Stone's voice had the same effect. Faculty X forced you to see the world from the rearview mirror, as it were. Smithy trusted his instincts and every time Stone spoke, they were signalling a five-alarm fire.

"Well...not sayin' we're not interested," Wizard said smoothly. "But like Smithy said...there's a lot to unpack here. *Lot* to unpack. And it's not really something Smithy and I can decide on our own. We work as a team, as you know. Once we follow up with the rest of our group, we'll be in a better position to answer you."

"Ah yes, of course...your colleagues."

Your colleagues...that was another thing that had Smithy hard-pressed to keep his butt still.

Jingo and Brick should have been here way before now. The agreement had been that they would check out the western quadrant, then make their way to the House. Stone's people had assured them that they would quickly bump into someone who could give them a lift via sled. They had also made it clear that allowing them to traipse around New Eden unescorted was a sign of his trust, and how seriously he took their "partnership"—as though their future collaboration were a done deal.

But the two men were now nearly two hours late. Wizard had made excuses to visit the men's room twice now, so he could try calling them, but each time he returned, he'd given Smithy a quick, expressionless shake of his head. *Nothing.* To now, Stone hadn't asked about them or even mentioned them. Smithy would have been more at ease had the man been throwing around outright accusations of espionage.

"You know," Wizard said slowly, "one thing might help us on the decision-making is seeing those profiles of the folks you got working for you. Seems to me there was some talk of that early on." He gave the room a lazy once-over as though the profiles might be hiding somewhere, or drop down on him at any moment from the ceiling.

"Of course," Stone said. "Ms. Nakamura, do you have those folders?"

The Asian woman walked silently to a side table and picked two blue folders off the top, then came over and handed them to Wizard and Smithy, her face emotionless.

Each contained a sheaf of glossy papers containing a brief biography of each of Stone's people, along with a head-shot. Their credentials were impressive; Ph.Ds. from major universities, experience at several zoos, publishing credits ranging from articles in scientific journals to books to consultant roles on major documentaries. Nakamura's data was among the papers, and a number of other people of different nationalities and ethnicities, but no Rhiannon Merrimans that Smithy could see.

"And this is *all* of your people?" Smithy asked casually.

"Of course," Stone purred.

We know she's here, Smithy thought, glaring at the voice box as though it were Stone himself. *So why isn't she in your little photo album?* They could simply ask, of course, but it would be too easy for Stone to lie.

"I have arranged a tour of the grounds," Stone said. "I think you'll find it most interesting. Mr. Corben, I think our friends would appreciate it if you began with the Western quadrant. There's an excellent chance they will encounter their colleagues along the way."

"Of course," Corben said. He had short black hair and a muscular build. He didn't look like someone who enjoyed smiling. "The sleds are ready right now, if you gentlemen would care to come with me."

Wizard and Smithy followed him, nodding pleasantly at the other members of Stone's team.

Smithy darted a quick glance at the voice box on the table. *If that's what he sounds like*, he thought, *I wonder what the hell he* looks *like…*

***

Jingo strode over to the window and glanced out at the forest. It was getting dark outside. He wasn't getting any sense of the wyrms' presence; nor did he hear any sounds of trees being knocked down or enormous bodies crawling towards them through the forest. They had found a bank of switches and furiously blinking lights covering one inner wall of the Box. Did it control the infrasound devices they had been told about? It seemed likely; the other alternative, that the wryms might have left of their own volition, was somehow not very comforting. Even Category Threes weren't supposed to have that much self-awareness.

He narrowed his eyes, willing himself to be as open as possible to the subtle indicators of other cryptids. They were out there, alright; a lot of them. But there was nothing to suggest they were anywhere near the Box.

Still, there was *something*. He couldn't say for sure it was a cryptid, or even another human being. It nagged in a corner of his mind, refusing to let him alone.

Brick was sitting hunched over the small table, thoughtfully sipping a cup of instant coffee. A cupboard with various other dry and canned goods had supplied the coffee, along with a spigot that dispensed hot water.

"Don't you think we ought to get out of here?" Jingo asked. "I think the wyrms are gone, and you know Smithy's going to be freaking out. Besides, it's getting dark. I don't like the idea of walking around in these woods with no light." He also wasn't crazy about standing around while that almost-tingle in his back brain drove him crazy.

"I know. But we might not get another chance to look over any part of Stone's facility without his goon squad watching."

"Doesn't seem like there's much to see."

It didn't; besides the table and cupboard, a cot and the blinking panel, the Box was pretty much empty. But Jingo couldn't argue that this was an opportunity that shouldn't be passed up. He walked slowly around the room, lightly touching the walls.

"From ghoulies and ghosties and long-legged beasties, and things that go bump in the night..." he murmured. It was something Cap used to say under his breath, on their first missions. His mantra, they used to call it.

"May the good lord protect us," Brick finished, taking a last swig of coffee. He got up and began covering the opposite wall. His touch was rougher than Jingo's. As he moved along the wall, he went from touching the wood to rapping it lightly with his fingers, then, with a frustrated look, he gave it a light punch with his fist—then another, as looking though he were engaged in a mock-boxing match with it.

"Could swear I almost had something, just now," he murmured. "It was almost in range, then...pfft. Nada."

Jingo scratched at his light beard. "Right? I've been getting that since we came in here. Nothing threatening, nothing you can even put your finger on...but *something*. Think it's the ultrasound?"

"Could be. We don't know much about what that stuff does to the cryptids, let alone humans with Faculty X. Something's screwing with our phones, that's for sure. I can't get a signal, and Flynn said that wouldn't be a problem anywhere on the reservation."

"Yeah, dude, and you believed him."

Brick moved over to the cot and picked it up, scanning the floor underneath. He was about to put it down, when Jingo said, "Wait."

The something was coming at him again, harder than before, as though it had been waiting for Brick to lift the cot. Jingo got on his knees and began feeling at the floor boards. One was cut shorter than the others, and protruded a couple of millimeters above the others. He got his nails under it and prised it carefully away from the floor.

"Ho, ho, ho," he muttered. "Merry Christmas." A small spiral-bound notebook was in the space formerly occupied by the short board. "Careful," Brick said. "Remember where you lifted it from. Once we've eyeballed it, we should put it back right where we found it."

Jingo picked it up gingerly and opened it. The pages inside were filled with columns of neat, precise handwriting.

"What is it?" Brick asked.

"Hard to say. It's mostly numbers. And dates. Last one's like two months ago."

"Think it's legit? Like something one of Stone's flunkies uses to keep track of how many babies his giant spiders eat?"

"Not impossible, but why stick it under a floorboard? And this…" He plucked out a sheet of paper folded in fourths. The creases were dirty and the paper showed signs of having been folded and unfolded many times. He handed it to Brick.

"It's a map," Brick said, shaking the paper open. "Like, how *Boy's Own Adventures* is that?"

The map was a rough diagram drawn in sharpie. It showed a cluster of small, precisely drawn arrow-like shapes around a square labeled "B."

"For Box?" Jingo asked. "And those arrows are supposed to trees?"

Brick shrugged. "You asking me?" he said. "I flunked art."

Slightly to the left was a circle labeled "L" which Jingo guessed to be a representation of the wyrms' lake. Dotted lines threaded around and between the trees, leading past them on the right to a large X, stationed between two trees larger than the others.

"And that's where the rainbow ends, huh?" Jingo asked. "Where the pot of gold is buried?"

"Unless Stone's collecting leprechauns to go with his dogmen, we have no way of knowing," Brick said, taking out his phone. After smoothing out the map on the floor he snapped two quick pictures of it. Then a third pic of one of the book's pages. That done, they slipped the map back into the book and hid it under the board.

"There," Brick said, stepping on the board to press it in and sliding the cot back over it. "Now let's go treasure-hunting."

ELEVEN

When they heard the sleds roaring towards them, the crypts froze, then moved gracefully into every available hiding spot, slipping behind trees, tall standing stones and the shadows they cast. Rhiannon had seen troupes of 'squatch do something similar before, and also dogmen once or twice. They knew how to hide themselves, that was for sure.

As for herself, hiding was the last thing she wanted to do. This was her chance, and she intended to take it. She ran towards the trail and stepped into the middle of it, waving her arms. When she heard the rough step of the big male 'squatch stepping out of hiding and quickly unhitched her wand.

"No!" she shouted. "Go on, get back!" Facing down a whole mob of cryptids was one thing; she liked her chances of scaring off a single 'squatch much better. She thumbed the wand's "on" switch, wincing at the sudden throbbing waves of ultrasound. The frequencies had been carefully set so that they caused humans minimum discomfort, though she suspected she was going to have a hangover-level headache the next morning. The 'squatch clearly didn't like it; he stumbled backward, baring his tusks and swiping at his head as though he'd suddenly contracted a throbbing migraine. The others moaned from the shadows, but none of them, Rhi noticed, moved from their hiding spots.

The noise of the approaching sleds became louder, and she turned back to face it, careful to keep the wand stretched out at arm's length. She waved her free hand at the sled, already looking forward to getting back to the House and enjoying a hot mug of brandy-laced coffee. But as the sleds came nearer, she realized something was wrong.

They weren't stopping for her.

There were two of them, one rocketing along behind the other. She could see Corben on the first, a lanky man she didn't recognize seated just behind him. Nakamura was piloting the second; a bearded black guy at her back. As they neared, Corben gave her a wide-eyed stare, as though she were a ghost. Then, just as Rhi laughed and gave him a wave, he veered sharply to the right. Nakamura followed suit, her mouth tightening. Soon they were past her and shooting down the trail, their passengers turning their heads to give Rhi quizzical stares. A moment later they were gone.

Rhi nearly threw her wand down in frustration. *What the hell?*

***

"Who was that?" Smith yelled, cupping hands around his mouth.

Corben didn't respond. Smithy knew better than to think the other man hadn't heard him for the wind. He shot a glance at Wizard, who raised his eyebrows.

"*Rhiannon*," he mouthed. Smithy had never been great at lip-reading, but there wasn't much doubt what his partner had said. And Smithy agreed with him. He slumped in his seat, thinking.

Okay, for some reason the Senator's daughter has become persona non grata among Stone's people. Now why do you suppose that is? Why didn't he just hand her her walking papers and let her go home? Maybe she knew something Stone didn't want getting outside New Eden.

Corben gave Nakamura a signal and the sleds slowed to a halt. Corben got off and walked off into the trees, speaking quietly but urgently into a phone. Smithy and Wizard turned to face Nakamura.

"Who was that we passed?" Smithy asked her. "I asked your partner, and I guess he didn't hear me."

"Not part of the tour," Nakamura said, shaking her head. "I'm not authorized to say any more than that."

Smithy traded glances with Wizard. "Alright," Wizard said, turning and walking, hands in pockets, up the trail. Smithy followed him, old leaves crunching loudly under their feet.

"Wait a minute," Nakamura said, following them with a quick, tight stride. "Where do you think you're going? These woods are dangerous!"

"And dark, and deep," Wizard said, not looking back at her. "That's why we're going back this way. What kind of gentlemen would we be if we let that lady back there by herself?"

Smithy heard Nakamura calling Corben, then, cursing quietly, taking something from her belt with a low click. "Okay, I need you both to freeze. Put your hands up. Now."

"She's got a gun on us," Wizard remarked in an off-handed voice.

"I know," Smithy said. He turned to face Nakamura. He saw Corben approaching, still speaking into his phone while keeping a cold eye on them. "Folks, I'm going to say this once. We're going to back to see what the story is with that woman. End of story."

"Don't think so," Corben said. "What you're going to do is come back with us. Tour is now over. Mr. Stone is not going to be happy with you."

Wizard sighed, turning to face Stone's people. "You know, Mr. Smith, I've heard that tone all my life. Never much liked it."

"What tone is that, Mr. Evermore?"

"That 'we're gonna tell teacher on you' tone. 'Cause that's what it is. Mr. Corben here probably thinks we're shaking in our boots, but to me he just sounds like a little bitch."

"I'd be inclined to agree with you, Mr. Evermore."

"Giving you one more chance," Corben said coldly. "No more talk. Here's what's going to happen...I just now called the House and we've got a vehicle coming out here that's going to take us all back. I don't trust you not to try anything funny while we're on the sleds. Then I'll let Mr. Stone deal with you."

"You in agreement with your colleague there, Ms. Nakamura?" Smithy asked. "Notice you've been mighty quiet while he dishes out the orders."

Nakamura glanced at Corben—it was only for a second, but Smithy caught it. Her lips were pursed, her eyes unreadable. *She's not scared of him, maybe, but she defers to him. They may be getting it on in the small hours, or maybe not, but he's definitely the man in their relationship, either way.*

The sudden sense of a cryptid nearby—and getting closer—hit Smithy at that moment, suddenly. From the way he started, he could tell Wizard caught it too.

"Well, will you take a look at this," he whispered.

Something tall and dark was thundering down the trail. It looked misshapen, having something of the same top-heavy look a mothman did, but less slender in the middle. It was difficult to see in the darkness but as it drew closer, Smithy saw it was Rhiannon Merriman, sitting astride the 'squatch's neck and riding it like a horse.

"Damn you, Corben, what the hell? Why didn't you stop for me?" The 'squatch's thundering stride made her voice jerk as her teeth clicked together.

"Shit!" Corben barked, dropping to one knee. He aimed at the creature, squeezing off a shot. At the last second, the 'squatch jerked to one side, missing the bullet. It continued thundering on, the sudden movement nearly causing Rhiannon to lose her seat. She clung to its neck, her legs swinging wildly from side to side.

At the same time, Nakamura cried out, as though she had been hit herself. She lunged angrily at Corben, shoving at his shoulders and nearly knocking him off his feet. "You could've killed her!" she yelled.

"Back off, Kristy!" Corben snapped. He wasn't pointing his gun at her, but the tension in his stance suggested he wanted to be ready in case he changed his mind. "You heard Stone; alive or dead, she's not coming back."

Smithy ran up to the 'squatch, ignoring the quarrel. He stared up at the beast, focusing his attention on it. Faculty X didn't allow him to communicate directly with crypts, but it did allow him to amplify his thoughts and intentions. At the moment, he was sending strong calming waves. Much to his relief, they seemed to work; there had to have been a reason why it was carrying Rhiannon back to her fellow humans rather than doing the hokey-pokey on her face. The 'squatch stood quietly, breathing explosively through flared nostrils while Rhiannon managed to clamber from its shoulders to the ground without breaking a limb.

"You okay?" Smithy asked her.

The young woman looked peevishly at him. "I guess I'll live," she said. "Unless you're planning on shooting me too."

A sound of engines being gunned filled the air, and the 'squatch snorted at the smell of exhaust. Corben and Nakamura, their disagreement apparently forgotten for the moment, had hopped back on their sleds and were flying up the path. Wizard stood watching them with his hands on his hips. "This is getting better and better," he said. "Now in all likelihood Big Daddy Stone will be calling out the hounds on us. And us down half our team, without even a pea-shooter to hold 'em off." He shrugged and laughed. "Kind of like those odds."

"Any idea why your boss had Prince Charming over there ready to blow your head off?"

She gave him a quizzical look. "Uhm, who are you again?"

"I'm Smithy. Funny man over there is Wizard. If you're lucky, and your colleagues haven't put them in their grave yet, you may get to meet Jingo and Brick soon."

"Sure looking forward to that," she muttered. "And what did you say you were here for?"

"That gets complicated. Bottom line, Stone was trying to recruit us for your little operation up here. From what we've seen it's pretty impressive...if you leave out the part about the benefits plan including a bullet in the face."

Rhiannon glanced at the 'squatch. "I'm not sure about him, or why he's elected himself my one-man cryptid chauffeur service, but you sure managed to calm him down."

"For now, anyway. He's anxious and upset, and if I'm reading it right, most of that's directed towards your boss. We've got some questions for you on that, but we'd better get off this trail and find the other members of our team. Then we can figure out next steps. I'm thinking Stone's place won't be particularly safe anymore. Same goes for other members of your team."

"And what about them?" Rhiannon said, jerking a chin back up the trail. A number of shadowy figures of different sizes and shapes were advancing towards them.

Wizard lifted his chin, narrowing his eyes at the crowd. "I'm gettin' dogmen, few frogs—are those *frogs*? Yeah, frogs. Maybe a moth or two." He gave a low whistle. "Everything's Category Three, everything is giving off the same unhappy vibes."

"Yeah, so my question stands," Rhi said. "What do we do with them?"

Smithy shrugged. "What else? Invite them along for the party. I'm guessing as long as we keep them on our side, we'll be better off with them than without them."

Rhiannon sighed. "So, what are we waiting for? Let's start walking."

TWELVE

Thierry met Corben and Nakamura at the House's rear entrance. He nodded once and led the way inside, not speaking a word.

Nakamura watched him carefully. Like most members of staff, she'd never particularly liked the Frenchman, but her direct contact with him was limited. Right now, she was more worried about Corben, who strode ahead silently, not looking at her once.

She sighed. She and Corben had been close since she'd joined the team three years before. They had never hooked up, as other members of the team often speculated, but she had valued his expertise and professionalism. He'd had her back for a long time, and she was grateful for it.

Now that seemed to be going south in a big way. Direction from Stone had been clear: Rhiannon was no longer part of the team. She was on the way out. But she hadn't once thought that meant they were to take her out. That crap was strictly for the movies...wasn't it?

If it was, Corben had misread the directives rather badly. If not...she might need to start rethinking her time here. The work was fascinating, but not at the expense of a bullet in the head.

She watched the man move down the hallway in front of her. She wanted badly to talk to him, to demand an explanation, anything to put her mind at rest. But since the incident in the forest, she had thought more and more that there was nothing he could say.

Something else, too…they had already bypassed several conference rooms, Stone's preferred place for meetings with staff, where he could hide behind the AV device. Nakamura hadn't been down this hallway in some time, but she knew what was at the end of it: Stone's private quarters.

"Where are we going?" she asked. What she meant was, *where are you taking me*, but she wasn't going to go there, not right now.

"Stone wants a debrief," Corben said shortly. Even though she'd known, the confirmation made her cold inside. She'd seen the man in person only once before, but that had been enough.

You can just walk away from this, she thought. *Not even explain. Just turn around, go get your ditty bag and bug out of here.* But even as the thought came to her, she knew it was wrong. She'd *seen* things, including Corben trying to gun Rhiannon down in cold blood. And, not to forget, she had willingly cut off all contact with her family and friends.

Your hands are too dirty. Just listen to whatever Stone has to say. With luck, Corben will keep you out of it. Then you can figure out what to do.

Something deep inside her laughed. *Coward*, it said. But by then they had reached the suite of rooms that served as Stone's private quarters. *A coward would run right now*, she thought, though it didn't make her feel much better.

A nurse slipped out of the door, one of the blank-eyed young women Stone had watching his vitals and keeping him happy 24/7. She'd never heard the women referred to by any name other than "nurse." They were all attractive, all wearing a little too much in the way of lipstick and makeup. All wore an unwavering little half-smile that Nakamura found unnerving.

"He's ready for you," the nurse said, not so much as glancing at them as she stepped aside, granting them access. Corben didn't say a word, just pushed the door open and strode in. After inhaling deeply and marshalling her inner resources, Nakamura followed.

Behind the door, Stone's quarters were all tasteful furnishings and soft classical music. The walls were lined with loaded bookshelves and still-life paintings of Alaskan wildlife—the standard bear, salmon and wolves rather than cryptids. To the rear of the room, looking out onto a picture window that showed a green expanse of woodland, Jacob Stone lay on a hospital bed hooked up to a number of blinking, whirring machines. Another nurse stood motionless over him, listening attentively while he murmured to her.

Corben cleared his throat. "Mr. Stone?"

It was obvious that Stone was already aware of their presence. "Come in, Mr. Co-hhrben," he croaked. He lifted a claw-like finger and the nurse took it as a dismissal. She slipped past the two, giving Nakamura a glance that said, clear as words, *better you than me.*

Nakamura followed Corben to Stone's bedside. She really didn't want to; she had never liked being in the man's presence, even with him talking over a speaker. But she forced herself. *Sooner I get through this, the sooner I'll figure out how to get out of here.*

"I unders-stand," Stone said, coughing to clear his throat, "that there was an issue *tuh*-today."

Nakamura forced herself to look down at the figure in the bed. Based on pictures she had seen and what she'd heard, Stone had never been a handsome man. But those pictures had been taken years before the incident that turned him into what he was now.

Stone's face always reminded Nakamura of a wax sculpture that had been allowed to partially melt, then reset. His flesh was whitish and flabby, hanging in heavy wattles round his skull. He no longer had eyes, as such; the glass ones in his head now were top of the line, supposedly, crafted by highly-regarded optical surgeons in Switzerland. To Nakamura they still looked obviously artificial. Dead and stony. And she couldn't escape the idea that even though they were glass, Stone could still see. It was almost certainly a result of his habit of focusing on the direction your words were coming from; a simple trick, but all too effective.

Most of his teeth were gone, and, like his eyes, been replaced. The artificial set was white and strong-looking, a little too long, gleaming wetly in the artificial light. Nakamura had heard some of the nurses referring to him as "Ole Sabertooth" once, and she had wondered why. That was before she'd seen him for the first time.

"We've lost Merriman, sir. And the two Task Force men."

"Indeed? And-d-d how did *this-ss* come to be?" The old man sounded calm; deceptively so, Nakamura thought. Those strange eyes moved around the room, pretending to look at them both.

"It was my fault, Mr. Stone," Corben said stoutly. "Nakamura had nothing to do with it. I take full responsibility."

"Duh-*do* you, now? Ch-chivalry is not d-dead, apparently."

"I *will* bring them back, sir. As soon as we finish this briefing."

"Mr. Cohr-rben, you realize that this-s error could have c-catastrophic consequences for-r New Eden. Losing M-Merriman would be bad, but l-losing the Task Force's help could be quite literally reh-*ruinous*. Keeping their in-interest was es-essential to *my* interests. You don't understand the T-Task Force as I do. You haven't been ex-ks-ks-posed to the Faculty, as I have." Stone moistened his lips with a lizard-like tongue. "They're not like you and-*nand* I. They th-*think* differently.

"As of nuh-now, you are no longer emp-ployed by this es-stablishment, Mr. Corben. I am turning this issue-ue over t-to other, more kuh-*qualified* men. In the meantime, thuh-though you are no longer m-mine, I believe some d-d-disciplinary action is in order."

While Corben stuttered and flustered, apologizing and pledging on his personal honor to undo his blunder, Stone's claw touched a button on his bedside control panel. A chime sounded in the recesses of the building, and the nurse who had been tending to Stone earlier returned to the room. Nakamura assumed Stone needed something—his pillow fluffed, a drink of water...but as the woman moved behind her, Nakamura felt a prick in the small of her back. The pain was small at first, but quickly escalated to crippling heights. In a matter of seconds, she was on the floor, gasping as her lungs fought to keep breathing. The nurse's feet in their glossy pumps moved idly near her head. She had an urge to grab the woman's ankles, begging to have life and movement restored to her.

Somewhere over her, Corben was shouting. Hands—*his* hands?—were gripping her shoulders, shaking her ferociously. But by now she was feverish and she was shaking on her own, so hard her teeth rattled.

The last thing she was conscious of was Stone's voice. While she couldn't make out a thing Corben was saying, she could hear Stone clear as a bell.

"Take a good luh-look, Mr. Corben. It'll be the las-st you s-see of your c-colleague. I'll give you the ch-chance to make good on your-r promise to me, but unders-stand that this is not m-mercy on my part. Whatever the outc-come, you m-might rather I gave you the same speedy ex-ks-it as Ms. Nakamura here."

Everything around her was fading with extraordinary speed, like the way the sun set out here. A moment or two later, just long enough to remember her family, and Kristy Nakamura's exit was complete.

***

Brick and Jingo moved swiftly and silently through the dark forest. There were echoes of the presence of cryptids all around them, but for the moment, nothing more than that. All the more reason to move quickly. The night was growing colder, and they were glad for the heavy coats they had worn.

"What do you think's under that 'X?'" Jingo asked, speaking in sporadic bursts, as though timing his words to coincide with his footfalls...

Brick's heavy form shrugged. "Got my suspicions," he said, but nothing more. At that moment Jingo went still, his eyes narrowing. "'Squatch," he said. "More than one."

Brick stood motionless, picking up on the vibrations. "Damn it," he swore softly. "That's not just a family. That's a whole freaking clan. *Several* of 'em."

"Trees," Jingo said, and Brick moved with him, both slipping behind a couple of nearby spruce. They could hear heavy footsteps, and there were more than 'squatches among them. *Dogmen, a whole herd of unidentifiable Category*

Threes...what are they all doing together like this? It isn't normal for them to travel together like this. And for that matter, where in hell are they travelling to?

"Crap," Jingo said from his tree. Brick could see his thin form lift its head, like he was trying for a breath of fresh air. "Is that Smithy with them?"

Brick focused for a moment. "Is that a skinny no-good Carolina boy?" he shouted, all pretense of keeping quiet gone. "And his friend Wizard, can't be bothered to buy his round of drinks?"

"I heard that!" Wizard's voice called from the trees. "Keep talking over there, Dr. Brick, so I can come and kick that wide butt of yours."

Smithy and Wizard moved into the moonlight, followed by a third human figure, and a mass of shadowy forms that—if Brick's senses were correct—made up a good portion of known Category Threes. "Guess the meeting with Papa Stone didn't go as planned," Brick said.

"This is the breakout session," Wizard said, jerking a thumb at the cryptids. "And this," he added, nodding at the third figure, an auburn-haired woman wearing an exhausted, yet quizzical expression, "is Rhiannon Merriman."

"Can't wait to hear this story," Brick muttered. "So, I take it we've already worn out our welcome with the big man."

"Stone's men tried to shoot Rhiannon," Smithy said. "And we still have no idea why. I'm guessing we'll have a bunch of Stone's goons on our backs before long, so let's save the stories for later."

"Where are we going to go, though?" Rhiannon asked, as the group started walking. "He's got this entire place tracked. If we tried just walking outside the grounds, we'd probably take a bullet each before we got three steps."

No one answered her. They trudged along until finally Brick lifted a hand and said, "There. I see it."

"X marks the spot," Jingo added, pointing at two trees growing closely beside each other.

"One of these days I'm going to learn how to speak your language," Wizard said. "Because it don't make a damned bit of sense to me now."

"We found what we think is some kind of treasure map," Brick said, making for the place he'd indicated. "Though it might not be *treasure*, exactly."

Smithy scuffed at the spot with his boot. "And we're going to dig this up...how, exactly? I don't know about you, but I didn't bring a shovel."

"Don't look at me, man," Wizard said. "I just got a manicure."

The biggest of the 'squatches, flanked by several dogmen, shuffled over and began tearing at the ground. The humans stood back respectfully as the cryptids made the dirt fly.

When they'd finished, they'd uncovered what looked like a dusty collection of bones, lying beside a bulging cloth sack. The skull was narrow and protruding, with long fangs jutting from the jaws.

"The hell is that?" Brick asked.

"Oh my god," Rhiannon said. She went to the hole and, after making placating gestures to the cryptids, lifted the sack. Pulling open the drawstring bag she looked in and gasped. "Jewels! One of our guys got killed by dogmen earlier. He had a sack of jewels just like this."

"Told you it was a treasure map," Brick said.

"Let me see one of those." Jingo reached into the bag like he'd been offered a piece of candy, pulling out a heavy piece of milky crystal. "Diamond," he said. "And big. If everything else in the sack is half this good, we're looking at a fortune."

"What's with the dogman, though? It's been there a while, and I have a feeling it didn't just die sitting on those stones like a broody hen. It was *put* there."

"I think I know the answer to that," Wizard said. "It was buried with the jewels to serve as a guardian. There's been a lot of speculation about cryptids being used as guardians for buried treasure. Not something you'd see on the Nature Channel documentaries."

"Wait, you mean like ghosts are said to guard hidden treasure?" Rhiannon demanded. She shook her head. "That's crazy."

"When it comes to this kind of thing, it's hard to draw the line," Smithy told her. "I think we should rebury this stuff. Somebody knew it was here, or they wouldn't have drawn that map. We know it's here now too. That's good enough for right now."

"Guys? I think we got company," Jingo said suddenly.

The sound of sleds growling as they closed the distance between themselves and their prey became impossible to ignore. They could make out a good six of them, each one carrying two helmeted riders.

"Alright, gentlemen," Smithy said. "Let's get ready to dance."

END